Morgan and
the Forty Thieves

Morgan and the Forty Thieves

A Magic Math Adventure

Book One

Written by Addie Abacus
Illustrated by Elisabeth Alba

PHANTOM HILL PRESS

Text Copyright © 2018 Patricia Tobin
Illustrations Copyright © 2018 Elisabeth Alba
Edited by Laura Morawitz

For more information on this book and the Morgan series, and for free access to an extensive Teacher/Parent Guide please visit www.addieabacus.com.
Published by Phantom Hill Press

ISBN 978-1-7328813-1-0

Typesetting services by BOOKOW.COM

Note on Getting the Most out of this Book

Answers to math questions are given in the story, so if you have fun figuring out the answer for yourself, pause at the illustration before continuing the story.

When you see a word or phrase in bold with a picture of a Medallion at the end of the sentence, it means there is more information on the subject available in a section called Medallion Matters at the end of the book.

For more information and a Teacher/Parent Guide, please visit www.addieabacus.com.

"The universe cannot be understood unless one first learns the language... It is written in the language of mathematics..."

Galileo Galilei

Barber Mansion, Massachusetts
1899

CONTENTS

Chapter One

THE NEW BOY

*"What is the pattern that connects
all living creatures?"*

Gregory Bateson

MORGAN felt a wet kiss on her cheek and woke up. A young beagle, not quite a year old, stood above her on the bed. Morgan reached up to scratch behind the puppy's soft ears.

"Morning Jip," she yawned as she sat up.

She blinked and looked around her. Gone were the flower curtains, the big boxes of toys, and the view of the gardens from her window. In their place was a bare room with an old dresser, plain white walls, and no windows at all. This time when she blinked, it was to hold back tears.

"I forgot we were here."

Jip licked Morgan's face, and she smiled, feeling a bit better. She wondered if she would ever see her home again: her beautiful bedroom, the gardens, the stables, the horses, especially her pony, Bailey. She missed Bailey most of all.

"At least I still have you, Jip," she sighed as she stroked her puppy.

Jip bounded off the bed and stood, wagging his tail. Morgan threw back her covers and went to the basin on the dresser. The floor was cold, and she stood on her tiptoes, shivering. Pouring water into the basin from a cracked jug, she leaned over to splash her face clean. Morgan's mother walked in through the doorway.

"I thought I heard you," her mother said, "Let's go up to the kitchens, my sweet."

Morgan gaped at what her mother was wearing—a simple ankle-length dress with a long white apron. Morgan had never seen her mother dressed that way. She was usually so stylish. Stooping to hold onto Jip, Morgan kept her face turned away from her mother's. She was trying to be brave, but so many things were changing so fast.

Hoping to match her mother's cheerful voice, Morgan said, "We're coming!"

She couldn't fool her mother though, who came into the room and stooped down to ruffle Jip's ears.

"It's been hard, I know," she said softly to Morgan.

Morgan couldn't bring herself to speak. She was trying not to let her mother see her tears.

Her mother looked at Jip and then gently at Morgan.

"I don't think Jip will be welcome in the kitchens. Why don't you take him to the gardens and let him run for a while, then leave him out back." Her mother paused, "I'm sorry, Morgiana, but I must go." She kissed Morgan on the top of her head, got up quietly, and left.

Morgan looked sadly at Jip. "And now I don't even get to have you with me."

⇒≫⋘⇐

Walking with Jip through the back gardens, Morgan discovered a maze of pathways heavy with the scent of moist earth and lilacs. A large granite fountain covered in moss and rust-colored lichen caught her eye. At its center, intertwined dolphins spouted water from their mouths, the spray arcing over tiny lily pads.

Morgan dipped her fingers into the cool waters of the fountain, startling small goldfish that sparked orange as they darted away. She wiped her hand absently on her dress. Following the example of her mother, Morgan had pulled on the simplest outfit she could find—a plain off-white frock with a forest green pinafore on top. It was for playing outside, so she thought it would work for the kitchens. She'd also pulled on stockings to stop her shivering, but now that she was outside, she hoped that the bright sun might get hot.

Not that it will matter when I'm stuck in the kitchens, she thought glumly.

As she continued, Morgan gazed at an area devoted to bright red roses. A hedge bordered them and surrounding each bush were white, rounded stones, making the bushes stand out against the light background underneath. She could tell that there was a pattern to the display of flowers, but it was hard to see from where she stood.

Patterns in everything, she thought. That is what her father taught her. He said there were patterns in the clouds, the waves of a pond, the colors of a rainbow.

"All of nature moves to the music of *math*, my bright one," he would say. *My bright one* he called her as her mother called her *my sweet*.

Morgan followed a path as it dipped under a long archway laced with vines. Along the borders, the ground was covered with periwinkles, one of her father's favorite flowers.

She stooped to cup a periwinkle in her hand. It was dark purple and still damp from the dew. She remembered a counting game her father played with her using the flower petals.

Each flower had five petals. Morgan began to count by fives.

"Five, ten, fifteen, twenty, twenty-five," Morgan counted aloud, as she pointed to a line of flowers.

Morgan's father had talked about the math found in flower petals.

"Did you know that almost all flowers have a certain number of petals?" he would ask. "There's a pattern to the numbers they have, and in a sequence, they go like this: **3, 5, 8, 13, 21, 34, 55, 89. . .**"

On and on, he would ramble with excitement. Morgan did not understand everything he said, but she loved it when her father spoke of his love for the pattern in things, and in turn, she learned to love numbers and patterns as he did.

"Numbers can be counted on," Morgan's father would say with a laugh. Morgan missed him so, so much.

When's he coming home? she thought.

A familiar ache rose inside her as Morgan tried to picture him on the Galapagos Islands, but she had trouble imagining much more than rocks and tortoises. Her father and a team of scientists were there to follow in the footsteps of a man her father described as **"one of the greatest thinkers of our time."**

Suddenly, her daydream was interrupted by a loud snarl from Jip, followed by wild barking. Morgan spun around and saw Jip chasing something—a big, dark animal—huge. It looked like a wolf. Racing through a small opening in the hedgerow bordering the garden, Jip and the animal disappeared. Morgan gasped and ran after them, scared that Jip would be hurt.

"Jip, come back! Stop!" she cried.

Morgan ran around the end of the hedge. Maybe she could catch Jip on the other side. As she was running, she heard the rumble of distant thunder. When she came around the hedge, she saw Jip still barking, but the wolf was nowhere in sight.

Instead, she saw only a boy who appeared to be a bit older than she was, flopped on the ground. He was thin with red, curly hair, and masses of freckles. As the boy got up on all fours, something on a leather cord around his neck swung toward the ground. It looked to be a strange set of copper circles, like a medallion of some sort.

Jip was barking directly at the boy who cocked his head to one side, considering the animal. "Whoa, boy. I'm not your enemy," he said to Jip.

Jip just increased his barking as the boy stood up unsteadily. He was taller than she was. His clothes were well-made but streaked with dirt. Though his trousers had a careful crease down the middle, they were also torn at the knee. His collar was starched, but his blouse had buttons missing.

He's well cared for, but they let him run wild, Morgan thought, and she liked him immediately. Maybe it was the way he looked at her, open and friendly, and grinning as if there was a ready joke on the tip of his tongue.

The boy eyed Jip, who was still barking, and then he began to bark right back. The dog paused, looking confused, and then barked even more furiously.

Smiling, the boy turned to Morgan. "Perhaps you can let him know that I don't speak *Dog*."

Morgan giggled and clapped her hands. "Jip! Jip, come here!" Jip stopped barking and trotted to her side.

"Sorry about that," she apologized. "He was chasing a wolf. Did you see it? Did it hurt you?"

The boy did not answer at first. Then he shook his head. "No," he said, "It didn't hurt me."

"Where did the wolf go?" Morgan asked.

The boy seemed unsure. Then he pointed toward the woods beyond the gardens. The two children stood in awkward silence for a bit.

"You must be the new cook's daughter," he guessed.

That's true, Morgan thought. *But it still sounds very strange to hear someone say it.*

The redheaded boy limped over and put out his hand. Morgan thought he looked a little silly acting like such an adult, with his pants ripped and leaves in his hair, but she took his hand to shake it anyway.

"Clarence Russell Barber, but you can call me Rusty," he said politely.

"Morgiana Elika Worth, but you can call me Morgan," she copied him with a smile.

Rusty looked her over. "You don't seem like a servant."

"I haven't been one for very long," Morgan admitted.

"How long?"

"This is my first day, actually."

"Your first day? What were you before?"

Morgan thought about this.

"I was just a girl like any other," she said. "We lived in a big house." She looked at the enormous mansion just past his shoulder. "Not nearly this big. And we had beautiful gardens, and a stable, and all that."

Rusty was watching her closely as if he didn't quite believe her. "What happened?" he asked.

"Well, when my father, um, disappeared, we couldn't afford to keep the house."

"Wait, your father disappeared?" Rusty asked. "That's strange. My father disappeared too!"

The two children looked at one another for a long moment. "How did yours disappear?" Morgan asked.

Rusty started to explain, "He went away on an expedition. That's a—"

"I know what an expedition is," Morgan said excitedly. "It's an adventure where scientists and explorers go off to a faraway part of the world to gather information." She paused, a little confused by the coincidence. "I know because my father disappeared on an expedition, too."

Rusty looked surprised, and he whistled. "What are the odds?"

Jip startled them as he began to bark again—this time at a chipmunk that was making his way across the path nearby. Morgan tried to hold Jip back, but the beagle tore after him in pursuit, chasing the animal up a tree where he scolded Jip from a high branch.

Morgan turned back to Rusty and shook her head. "It's too much of a coincidence. Where was your father's expedition?"

"The Galapagos," answered Rusty.

"I thought so," Morgan nodded. "They both must be lost on the same expedition."

Chapter Two

MAGIC SQUARE

*"Magic squares . . .
possess the charm of mystery."*

Paul Carus

MORGAN and Rusty walked back through the garden with Jip wandering in front of them.

"I don't suppose you have a lot of wolves around here," she said.

"Just approximately four hundred sixty-three and one half," the boy said with a smile.

Morgan smiled back. "One half?" she asked.

Rusty pointed to Jip. "That looks like one half to me."

Morgan laughed, and as they walked, she gestured toward the grand house. "They must know, don't you think that our fathers are on the expedition together?"

"My guess? Without a doubt," Rusty said. "But that's what we're going to find out for sure."

Morgan could see his mind was set, and she felt she had found an ally in this strange new place. She watched him as they walked together, being careful not to stare too openly. The two of them were like opposites—he was tall whereas she was small for her age. He was pale and freckled, and her skin was smooth and olive-toned. His hair was wild, red and curly, and her hair was straight dark brown. He chattered with ease as they walked while she observed him quietly. Then Morgan saw they were passing by the part of the garden filled with roses.

"Pretty patterns in the garden," she said.

Rusty looked surprised. "Most people don't notice," he said, and he stopped to look her over. "How old *are* you?"

"Nine," Morgan answered.

"I'm eleven," Rusty offered. "Come on—I want to show you something."

Rusty ran ahead, and Morgan followed down a short stair to a basement back door. Leaving Jip outside, they climbed a dark stairway just inside the doorway. The stairs went around in a circle and creaked loudly.

When Morgan stepped onto the floor above, it was like she entered another world. Facing a long hallway, Morgan saw a rich red carpet with multi-colored diamond shapes covering the floor. Morning light streamed in from an endless row of tall, paned windows. Rusty paused, listening at the top of the stairs. Morgan heard a heavy click-clack of heels on wood in the distance. Someone was coming up another stairway around the corner. Rusty motioned hastily for Morgan to follow him, and he hid behind a thick curtain. Morgan scooted in beside him just as the click-clack of heels got very close.

"The Dragon Lady," Rusty whispered, and then he put a finger to his lips. Morgan and Rusty stood very still behind the curtains, barely daring to breathe as the click-clack of heels abruptly stopped quite near.

I wonder who the Dragon Lady is? she thought.

Morgan felt like she had to sneeze, and she pinched her nose in alarm, trying to stop herself. Rusty watched her, and he clamped his hand over his mouth to keep from laughing.

The click-clack of heels started up again and moved away from them down the hall. In a whoosh of relief, the children let their breaths go and giggled from the pent-up excitement of hiding and not making noise. Sticking his head out from behind the curtain, Rusty dared to sneak a look down the hall, and Morgan peeked, too. She saw a tall, broad-shouldered woman wearing a dark ankle-length dress, walking stiffly away from them. Her hair was piled high on her head with gray wingtips swept back into a bun. It was the house-keeper, Morgan realized, the one who had met them late last night when they arrived. She remembered it had not been a warm welcome.

"Miss Stern?" she whispered to Rusty.

Rusty nodded. "The Dragon Lady. A word of warning, do NOT get on her bad side," he advised. Morgan nodded. Rusty moved over to a large window and gazed down, motioning for Morgan to follow. She walked over to stand next to him. This close, she could see the copper medallion that hung around his neck more clearly. It looked very old . . . ancient.

Before she could look more closely, Rusty leaned toward the window. As the medallion came away from his chest, she could see three very clear rings of white skin beneath where the medallion had touched him.

Three perfect circles, she thought.

Rusty looked at her, and Morgan shifted her gaze to the garden. "Oh!" she exclaimed.

She had never seen anything like it. A straight line of bushes bordered the garden, making a square. There were lines of bushes inside the square, laid out like a game of Tic, Tac, Toe. There were three squares across, three down, and three on the diagonal.

Garden Magic Square

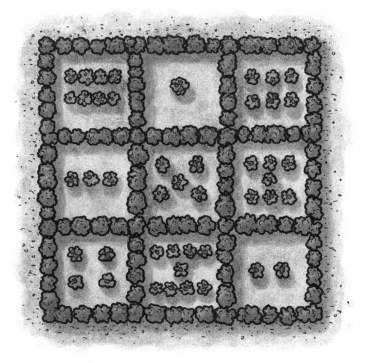

"This is called a **Magic Square**," Rusty said, pointing down to the garden. "The 'magic' is in the way the numbers—the number of bushes that is—work so well together. Can you see why?" ◉

Morgan gazed at the square, but before she began to think about the puzzle, she closed her eyes. Her parents had taught her a set of steps for quieting her mind when she was trying to figure something out.

She breathed in and out, in and out, slowly following her breath and allowing air and space to fill her. It was a form of focus that her mother's family had practiced for centuries.

When her thoughts settled down a little, she opened her eyes and looked at the garden again.

The bushes in each square almost looked like dots on dice, except some numbers went higher than six.

Rusty watched her as she studied the garden. "What do you see?" he asked.

"Well, the numbers of bushes inside the borders look kind of like dots on dice, and the lines of bushes inside the borders make me think of Tic, Tac, Toe," Morgan said.

"Not bad, not bad. Those are good clues to follow," Rusty said.

Morgan thought about Tic, Tac, Toe. The object of the game was to get three of the same symbols across or down or diagonally. Since the rows of bushes were neatly arranged, it was easy to see how many bushes were in each square.

She looked at the top row of bushes. There was a square with eight bushes, a square with one bush, and a square with six bushes. Then she thought about what Rusty had said: *The numbers work well **together**.* Another way of putting numbers **together** was to add them. Rusty might not have meant that, but it was a place to start. She began to add the number of bushes in each square across the top row.

8 bushes + 1 bush + 6 bushes = 15 bushes

Morgan looked down at her fingers to count and double-check herself when the numbers got too large. When she arrived at number fifteen for the total, she went on to the next row.

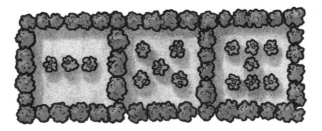

3 bushes + 5 bushes + 7 bushes = 15 bushes

She arrived at 15 again.

At this point, she became aware that Rusty was studying her face. She darted a glance at him, and he quickly looked away, but he had been staring at her eyes. Morgan knew that she was unusual looking—at least that's what people told her. They said she had her mother's eyes, which were large, almond-shaped and very green. Morgan glanced at Rusty again, and this time, a slow blush crept from his neck to his cheeks. Morgan tried not to smile so she wouldn't embarrass him more, and she looked back down at the magic square.

She added more rows of numbers: across, down, and on the diagonal. From time to time, she looked down at her fingers to help herself keep track. The result was always the same.

"Fifteen," she said. "The rows of numbers all add up to 15."

Rusty smiled at her. "Alright, I *am* impressed."

Morgan shrugged. "Sometimes, when I add up the bigger numbers, I still have to use my fingers."

Rusty shrugged back. "Whatever works."

"What a great secret!" Morgan said.

"This house is full of great secrets," Rusty promised.

Chapter Three

GRANDPA ALLEN AND THE WOLF

*"The most beautiful experience
we can have is the mysterious."*

Albert Einstein

"THERE'S someone I want you to meet," Rusty said.

Morgan followed Rusty down a long hall and up a grand stair-case. This upper passage had the same red patterned carpet, but instead of windows, the walls were lined with paintings warmly lit by gas wall lamps spaced between the artwork. Instead of the usual portraits of serious-looking relatives and ancestors found in most elegant mansions, these paintings were of all kinds of wildlife, so colorful and true that the animals looked like they might step right out of the frames.

Wishing she had more time to examine the pictures, Morgan passed a sleek panther, a preening peacock, and a massive elephant. A painting of a large wolf caught her eye, and she stopped in her tracks. It was so similar to the one she'd seen that morning. The wolf stood on the crest of a hill, looking into the distance as if it had just heard the howl of a pack member.

Morgan suddenly realized that Rusty was way ahead of her, poking his head into room after room looking for someone, then moving on. It was such a big house.

I could get lost in here, she thought.

Running to catch up, Morgan arrived at Rusty's side just as he reached a set of double doors at the end of the hallway. He put a finger to his lips and opened the door slowly. Peeking around the edge of the door, he opened it further and crouched down to sneak his way across the floor. Morgan stood in the doorway as she admired the room, which was by far one of the loveliest bedrooms she had ever seen. A four-poster bed draped with silver silk was on one side, with windows beyond that looked out over lush gardens and woods.

Rusty was slowly making his way toward a violet-colored sofa and two chairs that faced a fireplace. Sitting in one of the chairs was a thin, elderly man with bushy gray hair that stuck up at odd angles. When they walked in, the man was focused entirely on a necklace he held in his hands.

Morgan caught a quick glint of deep blue gems before the man slipped the necklace into his pocket. Rusty had nearly reached the older man's chair and was getting ready to pounce when the man said, without turning, "Rusty, would you please close the door, and then introduce me to our new guest?"

Rusty straightened and shrugged at Morgan, not surprised at all. The man stood and turned toward them, his face calm and friendly. He was perfectly dressed in tie, vest, and well-pressed trousers. His eyes were bright blue like Rusty's, and he had the same clear, open expression, except that his eyes were quicker—they missed very little.

He's a sly fox with a lot of secrets, Morgan thought. *Including the one in his pocket.*

Turning to Morgan, Rusty said, "Morgan, this is my grand-father. Grandpa, this is Morgan Worth, the daughter of the new cook."

As she walked up, the wiry man reached out his hand to her. "You may call me Grandpa Allen," he said kindly as she shook hands with him.

"Morgan and I have been talking," Rusty said, "and we realized—"

"That both of your fathers are missing off the coast of Ecuador, near the Galapagos islands?" finished Grandpa Allen.

He turned to Morgan. "When I heard of your trouble, I asked your mother to come and stay with us. She insisted on being a part of my staff, but she really need not work."

Morgan didn't know what to say. It sounded just like something her mother would do, but it was news to her.

Grandpa Allen continued, "Wonderful woman, your mother. And your father, Clayton, a very fine man as well. The expedition cartographer, I understand."

Morgan nodded. "Father says he became a map-maker because he loves the world from an eagle's point of view. He says it must be calm and peaceful, flying so high and looking down on the earth."

"Wise way of looking at the world, from so high up," agreed Grandpa Allen.

"Also, Grandpa," Rusty added, "I showed Morgan the secret in the garden."

The man was thoughtful as he looked at Morgan and then turned back to Rusty.

"How long?" Grandpa Allen asked him.

"Faster even than yours truly," Rusty admitted reluctantly, "but I was only seven then."

"Excellent. Excellent," replied Grandpa Allen. He stepped forward and studied Morgan, pinning her in place with his sharp focus. She felt a bit uncomfortable.

"Impressive for such a small thing," he declared.

There was a sudden series of shouts outside. Morgan, Rusty, and Grandpa Allen quickly moved to the windows, and Grandpa Allen opened one to give them a better view. A flock of crows flew in a startled circle in the far corner of the gardens. Then, from the same corner, a horse without rider or saddle burst from a hedgerow. Galloping in fright, it twisted this way and that, confused by the lines of bushes and hedges blocking its way. Morgan thought immediately of the wolf she had seen earlier, but what came running after the horse was a small man holding a harness. Grandpa Allen moved toward the hall, and the children followed.

✦

When they arrived at the back door and stepped outside, they could see the horse still moving anxiously, stalled in all directions by hedges. The stableman was trying to corner the animal, but it was too jumpy.

Morgan made a quick decision. "Where are the kitchens?" she asked Rusty. He pointed down a hallway behind them. Morgan ran as fast as she could and burst through the kitchen door. Her mother whirled around from the stove as Morgan lunged forward and grabbed a carrot from the table.

"Morgan!" her mother cried.

Miss Stern stepped into the kitchen from a side pantry. She glanced at Morgan and folded her arms, but just as she was about to say something, Morgan turned and ran.

Uh Oh, Morgan thought. *Looks like I might already be on the Dragon Lady's bad side.*

Having no time for explanations, Morgan ran out the door to join Grandpa Allen and Rusty in the garden. Rusty was nowhere to be seen, but Grandpa Allen was slowly making his way toward the scared animal.

Morgan passed him running, cautiously slowing down as she came closer to the horse. She held out the carrot, making gentle sounds as she moved forward. By this time, the stableman had blocked off the opposite end of the row from Morgan and Grandpa Allen. It took some time for the beast to calm down, but after a while, it became curious about the carrot Morgan held. The horse finally walked up and sniffed at the carrot.

Grandpa Allen was watching it all carefully, and he smiled when the horse began nibbling the carrot.

"And good with animals, that is important," observed Grandpa Allen to himself.

Morgan's mother came out the back door, hurrying toward them, unaware of the drama that had just taken place.

"Morgan, what are you doing? I expected you in the kitchens ages ago," she said. Turning to Grandpa Allen, she said, "I'm sorry, sir."

"No need to be sorry, Dara, and please, I ask you again to call me Allen. As for Morgan, she has actually just saved the day, and I think her talents would be better used outside the kitchens. Can you loan her skills to me for a time, please?" he asked.

While Dara considered Grandpa Allen's request, Morgan soothed the horse with strokes along his neck. The man from the stable came up and hooked a harness over the horse's head. Grandpa Allen gestured, and the stableman walked the horse over to him. Morgan patted the horse as she watched Grandpa Allen and her mother, and saw that their differences were striking.

Grandpa Allen towered over her mother. He was scraggly like a scarecrow, with pale, wrinkled skin and rumpled gray hair. Her mother, on the other hand, was tiny, with smooth, olive skin, and dark hair caught back in a neat bun.

Dara looked from Grandpa Allen to Morgan, not knowing quite what to say. "If you think she could help you, sir —I mean—Allen." Dara seemed embarrassed to be using Grandpa Allen's proper name.

"Thank you, Dara," said Grandpa Allen. "She's already proved to be useful, and I am delighted to have you both here."

Dara sighed and relaxed a little. "Thank you for having us. I'll be in the kitchens cooking supper."

"And that would be?" Grandpa Allen asked, hopeful.

"A surprise," replied Morgan's mother with a lovely smile.

Morgan and Grandpa Allen walked the horse toward the stable. As they rounded the last row of hedges, they could see another group of horses running loose in the far fields. The horses shied away from a dark form that was chasing them.

"It's the wolf!" Morgan shouted to Grandpa Allen, but he didn't look as alarmed as he should. She froze, watching the horses as the wolf pursued them without knowing what to do.

It will catch one of them! she thought panicked. *Why isn't Grandpa Allen doing anything!*

Morgan was trying to get up the courage to dart toward one of the horses when she noticed something puzzling. The wolf seemed to be chasing the horses, but never catching any of them. And the wolf was enormous—a much more powerful runner than the horses. It could catch them easily, but it wasn't. Something clicked in Morgan's head as she watched the wolf. She saw it wasn't chasing the horses at all.

It's herding them, like a sheepdog, Morgan realized.

It couldn't be, she thought mystified. *Wild animals don't act that way.*

Every time one of the horses would make a break for the outer field, the wolf would casually lope over and cut it off, forcing it to turn back toward a riding ring. Morgan watched with surprise as the wolf eventually forced the horses into the ring.

Grandpa Allen walked right past her toward the wolf.

He's acting like it's just a big dog or something, Morgan thought.

But it wasn't a dog. The wolf was far too large—about the height of a miniature horse, with paws the size of dinner plates. It was covered in dark fur except for a patch of white on its chest.

As Grandpa Allen neared the beast, she braced herself for violence. She expected bristling fur, snarls, charging, and snapping jaws. Instead, the wolf stood there calmly, leaving Morgan bewildered by the animal's unusual behavior.

Grandpa Allen reached the riding ring and closed the gate on the horses. The wolf turned and loped into the far fields.

Soon only the tall grasses could be seen moving in a ruffled wave, and then there was nothing to be seen—as if the wolf had never existed.

Chapter Four

Puzzles and Passages

*"Pure mathematics is . . .
the poetry of logical ideas."*

Albert Einstein

"How did the horses get loose? And *where* is Rusty?" Morgan asked as she and Grandpa Allen were returning to the bedroom where they had met. She was munching on a bread roll she had grabbed from the kitchen.

Grandpa Allen seemed preoccupied, and he didn't answer right away. When they rounded the corner in sight of the bedroom, Morgan saw Rusty waiting outside the double doors.

He looked even worse than the first time she'd seen him. He was short of breath, and his face was sweaty and red with a slash of dirt across his cheek. While his clothes had been dusty before, now his pants were encrusted with mud.

"Where did you go?" she asked Rusty as they arrived at the doors.

"I was just, uh," Rusty glanced at Grandpa Allen, and then continued, "chasing another horse that ran into the woods."

Grandpa Allen took out a set of keys and unlocked the double doors to the bedroom. Morgan had noticed when they left earlier that despite their rush to get the horses, he had stopped to lock the doors. At the time, she thought it was strange, but then she remembered the gemstone necklace and decided he might have other valuables in the room.

Grandpa Allen pushed open the double bedroom doors, waving Morgan in first. She gasped at what she saw.

The bedroom was in shambles. Every drawer was pulled out, and every cushion flung to the floor, along with sheets and quilts. In one corner, glass fragments from a smashed wall lamp lay scattered across the floor. Pictures from the mantle above the fireplace had been tossed to the ground and trampled. There was no place left in the room that wasn't a mess.

Rusty stuck his head in behind her and whistled. "I see you've redecorated."

Morgan turned back to Grandpa Allen and saw him pat his pocket where he'd hidden the blue gem necklace. He saw Morgan watching him and put his hand back down by his side.

"It looks like someone was searching for something," Morgan said.

"Several someones I would think," Grandpa Allen said, as he pulled twice on a silken cord hanging from the ceiling. "We weren't gone that long."

Morgan found the timing suspicious. How had this happened at the exact moment when the horses had escaped? Morgan remembered a riddle her father had told her when she was young.

"Bears, Bees, and Frogs are three animals that don't seem to have much in common," he told her one autumn when she was very young. "But at about the same time of year, they all disappear, and then much later, they all return. In the period they are gone, there is a change outside—it is winter. Do you think these two events have something in common?" he would ask.

When she was older, he explained that his little stories were logic puzzles designed to help her think about the world around her and the patterns that connect things.

Again, she thought about the horses and the ransacked room. Somehow the horses had gotten out of their corral. While they were all gone taking care of the horses, the place had been ransacked. It was possible the two events were not related, but not likely.

"The horses might have just been a diversion," Morgan guessed.

"I'm with her." Rusty jabbed his thumb at Morgan.

Grandpa Allen glanced between them. "My thoughts exactly," he agreed.

There was a gentle knock at the bedroom doors. An elderly gentleman dressed in a black and white uniform stepped inside. Wrinkles lined his face, and his watery eyes sat deep within their folds. As he took in the dreadful mess of the room, he teetered a little, and one hand reached for the door handle to steady himself. He ran the other over his carefully combed wisps of hair in what seemed to be a habitual gesture.

"What happened in here, sir?" the uniformed man asked.

"We're not certain yet, Mr. Grennan," Grandpa Allen said. "Have there been any visitors this morning?"

"No, sir, Mr. Barber. Been dead quiet 'round here lately. 'Cept for the horses gettin' out," the man said. "And, and . . . " The elderly man trailed off—too upset to know how to continue.

"It's alright, Mr. Grennan, I don't hold you responsible for this chaos. Would you please have the staff check all doors and windows on the ground and cellar floors to see if any are broken open?" asked Grandpa Allen. "And please ask if anyone saw someone or something unusual this morning."

Mr. Grennan seemed to recover and stood a little straighter. "Yes sir, right away, sir, and I'll send up Enid and Lottie to clean, sir," the elderly man offered.

"Not to bother. The children and I will clean this up," Grandpa Allen assured him. Mr. Grennan nodded and shuffled away.

"Poor Mr. Grennan. I do believe this mess has given him a fright," Grandpa Allen said. "He's been with me since I was quite young. I used to call him 'old stuffy,' though, now that I think back on it, he probably wasn't even very old back then."

Morgan walked to the bed and began to pick up the covers from off the floor. Rusty joined her to help.

"Later children," Grandpa Allen said, moving toward the fireplace, "We have more important things to look into right now." He turned to Morgan. "But before we go on, I have a riddle of sorts for you, child."

"My father and I used to play with riddles all the time," Morgan said, as she placed the covers on the bed.

"Alright, then." Grandpa Allen moved quickly as he spoke, wasting no time as he presented his riddle to Morgan. He went to a nearby desk and pulled the glass globe from an oil lamp, talking all the while.

"All the doors and windows of this house are locked. While I have not yet converted all parts of this house from oil and gas lamps to electric, I have wired up an alarm system. An alarm is triggered when any locked outside door or window is opened. Yet when someone broke in this morning, no alarm was triggered."

"Now the door to this room was also locked, and only I have a key. So, how did the people who ransacked this room get in?" Grandpa Allen searched in a drawer for matches and lit the wick, then replaced the glass globe.

Morgan was thinking through his question.

"Could someone have cut or disabled the alarm system? Or could it simply be broken?" she asked.

"Not bad guesses, Grandpa," said Rusty, and then he explained to Morgan, "The thing is if you cut any wires, it sets off the alarm."

"And I checked the system myself just this morning," Grandpa Allen added.

"Also, this door was locked. So how did they get in here?" mused Morgan.

She practiced quieting her thoughts, breathing in and out. What popped into her head was Rusty telling her that the house was *full of secrets*.

"Could there be a secret way out of this room that leads to a secret entrance from outside—one that wouldn't have a locked door?" she asked.

Rusty shook his head in wonder. "You sure you're only nine?"

Without answering her directly, Grandpa Allen handed Rusty the lamp and walked over to a large vanity table near the bed.

He carefully pushed the vanity aside and stood facing the large mirror, which had hung over it. Reaching up, he pressed several spots along the gilded edge of the mirror. Then he hooked his fingers around the mirror frame and pulled back, swinging it open like a huge cupboard door, revealing an abandoned closet. The musty scent of stale air wafted over them.

Morgan watched Grandpa Allen step awkwardly over the section of wall that had been behind the table. He then pushed hard at the closet's back wall, and another secret door opened into deep blackness beyond. Despite having guessed the secret already, Morgan was still shocked and terribly excited.

I never thought I'd see a real hidden passage! she thought.

"I'll go first," said Grandpa Allen, "Then Rusty with the lamp, and then you can follow, Morgan. Be sure, please, to close both the mirror and the door after you, as very few know of this secret passage."

Morgan nodded as she took the lamp from Rusty while he climbed over the section of wall and then handed it back to him. He turned to join Grandpa Allen, and the two of them were swallowed up in the dark. Taking a deep breath, Morgan stepped up and over the wall into the closet, carefully pulling the mirror closed behind her.

Chapter Five

FOLLOWING THIEVES

*"A mathematician is a blind man
in a dark room
looking for a black cat
which isn't there."*

Anonymous

MORGAN stepped into the dark passage and saw Grandpa Allen and Rusty squatting on the floor with the lamp. They were examining a broad set of muddy footprints.

Morgan knelt next to them. She could see that there were different sets of footprints.

"How many thieves do you think there were?" Grandpa Allen asked Rusty and Morgan.

How many thieves were there?

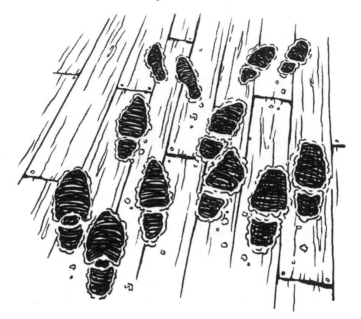

"I get five different people so far," Morgan said.

"With possibly one more over here," Rusty said, pointing to a corner. "That makes," he pretended to think, "Twenty-six?"

Morgan laughed despite her fears. It was creepy in the dark corridor, and the lamp Rusty carried lit their faces from below in a ghoulish manner.

"Okay, so there are about six of them," said Grandpa Allen. "We better go quickly if we hope to catch them."

Morgan watched Grandpa Allen and Rusty move off with the lamp. She hurried to keep up, not wanting to be left alone in the pitch black.

"What if we do catch up with them?" she asked. She was trying to be brave, but thinking about what kind of people they were following made her a little scared.

Rusty turned back, and when he saw her face, he took her hand and squeezed it. "Don't worry. I won't let them hurt you," he said, for once serious.

"You won't be getting near them, child," Grandpa Allen said. "I have another plan." He glanced at Rusty, who mysteriously nodded as if he and Grandpa Allen had just agreed on something.

So many secrets, thought Morgan, as they hurried along.

They rounded a sharp corner, and rushing wind blew out the lamp. Morgan heard Grandpa Allen curse softly under his breath.

"I'll put the lamp down on the ground at our feet," Rusty said in the darkness.

Morgan could hear them fumbling and the clink of glass and metal as she stood over them. It was so pitch black she couldn't see anything. Then light from a match flared.

"Why does the house have these secret passages?" Morgan asked as she watched them relight the lamp.

Grandpa Allen peered up at Morgan as he replaced the glass globe on the lamp. "I bought the house from an abolitionist friend of mine," he explained. "This used to be a stop on the **Underground Railroad** between the southern states and Canada."

"An abolitionist was a person who wanted the slaves to be free," explained Rusty. "The slaves would escape from their masters and move from safe place to safe place. All the houses and farms along the way were known as the Underground Railroad."

"Got a good price on the place, too," Grandpa Allen said. "He couldn't just sell it to anyone, not with the evidence that it was a safe house. Sadly, even in the north, many people do not treat former slaves well, or anyone who helps them."

They were watching and waiting for the wick of the oil lamp to catch a steady flame. There were still a few gusts of wind, and the light flickered.

"Mother says there were times when her family first came here that people thought she was a slave because of her darker skin," Morgan said. "They didn't treat her very well. Father said when they looked at her, they were blinded by prejudice, but he was blinded by beauty."

Grandpa Allen chuckled. The gusts of wind had stopped, and the air seemed suddenly still and heavy. Rusty and Grandpa Allen stood, and all three of them continued down the passage.

Reaching another sharp corner, Grandpa Allen turned to shield the lamp in Rusty's hands, but no blast of air greeted them. They found themselves at the top of a dank stairway, rickety with age, and discolored with mold. Clattering down, they entered a smaller tunnel. The ceiling was so low in spots that Grandpa Allen had to stoop. Earthen walls, like those of a cellar, surrounded them. It was much colder. Large boulders stuck out of the sides of the passage. At times the tunnel narrowed so much they had to go in single file, squeezing past the tight spots.

They walked through the tunnel for an awfully long time. Morgan's feet were cold, and she was starting to shiver when they came to a dead end. A wooden ladder led up to the ceiling where a thin streak of light shone through at the top. The rungs of the ladder were splattered with mud.

Grandpa Allen turned to Rusty. He was still stooping, and he looked tired and disheveled. "I'll go up first, and you children wait here until I call you."

"Don't you think I should go first?" Rusty asked.

"You are very skilled, my boy, but a bullet or knife can still hurt you. If you hear sounds of a struggle, I want you and Morgan to race back through the tunnel and alert the household of my whereabouts."

Rusty looked reluctant.

"I'm counting on you, and I want your promise," Grandpa Allen said.

Rusty let out a sigh. "Alright," he agreed.

Grandpa Allen went up the ladder too quickly and slipped on a muddy rung. He swore softly again, continuing more carefully. When he reached the top, he shoved aside something blocking the entrance to the tunnel. Climbing out, he covered the opening once more.

Morgan waited at the bottom of the ladder. It was stifling down in this dark hole, and as the minutes passed, she felt increasingly anxious. She listened with all her might but could hear nothing from above. She tried to put her mind on something else other than her worry for Grandpa Allen.

"What did he mean that you're skilled?" she asked Rusty. "Have you been trained to fight?"

"Something like that," Rusty said, not really answering her question. He traded the lamp to his left hand, wiping his right down his trousers, then squinted back toward the opening above them. "I worry about him because he's getting pretty old for this type of thing. He always tries to do too much, like he forgets his age or something. He's all I've got, you know? Now that father is lost."

Morgan nodded. "I keep telling myself that my father will be okay. Explorers get lost all the time, but it's been so long."

"I'm beginning to think too long," Rusty said sadly.

Morgan thought about her mother and how grateful she was to have her.

"Your mother?" she asked.

"She died when I was born," Rusty said. "It's only ever been me and father and Grandpa Allen. And now just Grandpa Allen, I guess," he added. "I have her picture," Rusty added.

Morgan looked at the medallion around his neck. He picked up the medallion. "Oh, not with me," he said. "It's back in my room. I'll show it to you when we get back."

Morgan didn't say anything. She looked again at the white marks on his chest underneath the medallion as Rusty held it up.

Three perfect circles, she thought again. *How strange that they would be so perfect.*

Rusty adjusted the lamp again to his other hand, and the lamplight flickered. Morgan watched him and thought about how hard it must be not to have a mother.

"Well, now that we are living here, you can share my mother if you'd like," Morgan said in a low voice. "She's awfully nice."

The two children were quiet for a moment, and then they smiled at each other.

The cover above was pulled aside, and light streamed down the ladder. Grandpa Allen leaned over the opening.

"You can come up!" he called. "Leave the lamp at the base of the ladder, Rusty."

Rusty blew out the lamp, then set it down and shook out his arms. Morgan climbed the ladder, and reaching the top, she looked around and pulled herself up onto the ground. They were in the middle of a small garden surrounded by woods. Flagstones led out from the center where they had emerged. The stones formed a circle pattern with benches and flowers lining the outside. At the edge of the circle was a lovely little fountain built out of stone that sparkled where the sun shone on the rock.

Morgan walked over to the fountain and dipped her hands in the cool trickle of water.

Rusty gestured toward the fountain. "That's the old spring. Grandpa says it's been here forever."

Grandpa Allen and Rusty worked together to move a large wooden octagon covered with a thin layer of stone, back over the entrance. When fully in place, the cover blended in so well with the other flagstones that she would never have known the opening was there.

"Can you get a scent?" Grandpa Allen asked Rusty as he dusted off his hands. Rusty glanced at Morgan.

Grandpa Allen seemed to catch himself, and then he said to Rusty, "Why don't you see what you can find?"

Rusty ran into the woods, and Morgan wondered again what was going on.

"Shouldn't someone go with him?" she asked.

"He'll be okay," Grandpa Allen assured her.

"I'm not so sure," Morgan said, and she began to run after Rusty.

"Morgan, come back!" Grandpa Allen called.

But Morgan was worried, and she didn't stop. She ran directly into the trees after Rusty. There was a distant rumble of thunder, and she glanced at the sky. There wasn't a cloud in it. As she came up over a small hill, she stopped in her tracks.

There, directly facing her, only a few feet away, was the same wolf she had seen before. Morgan took in his huge form, and then she noticed the patch of white on his chest. From this close, she could see circles of white against the dark black fur.

It can't be. Morgan thought. *Three perfect circles.*

Morgan and the wolf stared at each other. For some strange reason, she wasn't at all scared. She was more confused. The circles of white on the wolf's chest had sent Morgan's mind moving in many directions at once.

The wolf seemed to cock his head at her, and then in one clean leap, he was running away, disappearing into the dense woods.

"You frightened me, girl," Grandpa Allen said as he puffed wearily up the hill behind her.

Morgan could see how tired he was, and she felt bad about worrying him.

"I'm sorry. I just couldn't let Rusty go after those people alone."

"I understand how you feel," Grandpa Allen said, "but Rusty can take care of himself." He seemed about to say something else, but he hesitated.

"I saw the wolf again," she told him. "And I noticed something strange on his chest." Morgan watched Grandpa Allen closely for his reaction and then continued when he said nothing.

"It doesn't make any sense. I know there's a connection between Rusty and the wolf, but—" she paused, trying to explain how she felt, "It just doesn't make sense."

Grandpa Allen avoided Morgan's gaze. Morgan waited, still feeling confused. Then Grandpa Allen seemed to make a decision. He raised his eyes and looked directly at her.

"We seldom run across such strange happenings, and I can understand your confusion," Grandpa Allen said. "You've been raised by two brilliant scholars—your father a mathematician and cartographer by trade—your mother—she studied philosophy, didn't she?"

"And physics," Morgan said. "She is one of the first graduates from Radcliffe College. That's where my parents met when my father was an assistant professor."

"The situation we have here is part of the world that I would describe as 'unknowable', and while there is much that falls into that category, I've discovered in my life that certain things exist that are so unbelievable that a clever brain like yours might call them—" Grandpa Allen searched for a word.

"Impossible?" Morgan asked.

"Yes," he agreed simply.

Rusty ran up to them, breathing heavily. "Couldn't catch them."

When Grandpa Allen and Morgan didn't answer or turn to look at him, Rusty asked, "What's going on?"

"The jig is up, my boy," Grandpa Allen said to Rusty. "Morgan is far too smart to be kept in the dark. It would be disrespectful, an insult to her intelligence."

"So, we can tell her?" Rusty was delighted.

Grandpa Allen nodded. "It's quite a long tale, so may I suggest we return for our meal, and then we can gather in the bedroom where we started."

"Yes, please," said Morgan. "I've barely eaten all day."

Grandpa Allen grew very serious. "This story will be for your ears only, my dear. I hope you understand that we are going to share with you, and only you, one of our greatest secrets."

Chapter Six

TALE OF THE FORTY THIEVES

"Mathematics is the science of patterns."

Lynn Arthur Steen

MORGAN, Rusty, and Grandpa Allen finished putting the beautiful bedroom back in order just as Morgan's mother came in carrying a tray of tea and cookies.

"Dara, that meal was spectacular. What was the name of the dish again?" Grandpa Allen asked.

"They're called kebabs. My mother taught me to make them. She said it was the most common dish where she grew up," Dara explained.

"Uncommonly delicious!" Grandpa Allen exclaimed. "You will spoil me."

"It's the least I can do for all your kindnesses," Dara said. She looked around the room. "You all worked hard picking up. Have you figured out what the thieves took?" she asked.

Grandpa Allen hesitated. "I don't believe the losses were too great," he said.

"Thank goodness," Dara said, as she left the room.

The children and Grandpa Allen settled into the area facing the fireplace. It was very early summer, and a fire was lit to keep out the evening chill.

"What did the thieves take?" Morgan asked as she and Rusty flopped onto the sofa with Jip at their feet.

Grandpa Allen sipped his tea in the other chair. "I'm not sure, but I believe they did not find what they were searching for."

"What was that?" Morgan asked.

"Well, that is part of my story," Grandpa Allen said.

He gazed at the fire for a short time, waiting for the children to settle.

"Long ago, when I was a young man," began Grandpa Allen, "I worked as a servant in a household far to the north near the Canadian border."

"You were a servant?" asked Morgan.

"If you keep interrupting me, child, we will be here all night — since this is rather a long tale," said Grandpa Allen.

Morgan nodded quietly.

"Now, not only was I a servant but a very poor fellow indeed. I worked in the kitchens of a mansion and slept in a back hall with my older brother. One night we were left alone, my brother and I, with the caretaker. The master and other servants traveled to a neighboring town to stay with one of the master's relatives for a few days. Feeling restless that first night, I decided to wander the halls of the mansion. I was careful not to wake the caretaker as he would have beaten me for entering the private areas of our master.

"I was enjoying looking at all the items of luxury that were usually out of my reach when I heard the noise of glass shattering. It sounded like a downstairs window. Running to the landing overlooking the great entrance hall, I leaned over the rail. A dark shape shimmied in through a window and landed on the floor. I could see it was a man dressed in black. He hurried to open the grand front door, and in crept a large group of people who were also dressed in black. I counted them as they came in."

"How many were there?" asked Morgan, not able to stop herself.

How many thieves did he see?

"About forty, including the leader who was a huge, bald fellow. He motioned to a few men, and they went into a side bedroom where the caretaker was sleeping.

"Dragging the poor man out of bed, they gagged him and tied him up. They treated him roughly and threw him into the corner of the great hall. Then the leader spoke aloud and ordered the men to split up into groups of ten, one group for each floor. There were four floors in the house, including the cellar."

I could add 10 four times, Morgan thought.

$10 + 10 + 10 + 10 = 40$

Or I could just multiply 4 x 10 = 40.

"You were probably right then. There were about forty men," Morgan said. "Weren't you scared?"

"I was terrified," Grandpa Allen confessed. "I thought about my brother and the caretaker, but I couldn't get to either of them. My only chance was to hide. So, I ran down a hallway looking for a place to take cover. For the next hour or so, we played cat and mouse as I ran from hiding spot to hiding spot. When they got near me, I could see that they were mean-looking men as if life had been hard on them, and they had decided to be hard right back. They dressed in the kind of garments any outdoor laborer would wear, and their clothes weren't really all black, but in shades of grime. They all carried sacks with them and loaded only the most valuable goods they could find.

"When the thieves gathered to leave, I knew I had to do something. After they went out the front door, I ran downstairs and tried to rouse the caretaker, but he was unconscious. I ran to my brother, who was still asleep! He didn't believe me when I told him what I'd seen, but at least he agreed to check on the caretaker. I was losing time. With or without my brother, I was determined to follow the thieves.

"Running to the stables, I harnessed a small, sturdy Welsh pony, then rode hard to catch up with the thieves. At first, they moved quietly, but as they traveled further from the estate, they became noisier, and it was easy to follow them in the dark, despite the many side roads they were taking.

"After about an hour, they left a narrow back road, disappearing into a forest. I was cold and tired at this point. Under the trees, I could barely see a few feet ahead of me, so I had to follow them more carefully. I was afraid if they found me—"

Grandpa Allen stopped and gazed at the children.

"Let's just say," he continued, "that it was very important that I not be seen. We came to an area at the base of a cliff strewn with large boulders. I tied my pony behind one of the rocky outcrops and climbed on top to get a better view of the group. The thieves were unloading the bags of stolen goods from their horses and stacking them next to the cliff.

"The leader of the thieves brought out a large sack hidden behind a nearby boulder. Drawing stones from the sack, he began to place them in nooks in the rock wall. When he finished, he stood facing the cliff. Then he threw back his head and yelled something that sounded like 'Ah Bah Say Sum.' There was a huge cracking sound, like a lightning strike, followed by a BOOM of thunder. The cliff shook, and a giant rock slab slid aside, revealing a deep, dark cave."

Grandpa Allen paused and looked at his listeners. Morgan felt completely confused at this point. She glanced at Rusty, but he seemed unfazed like he'd heard it all before. She turned back to Grandpa Allen.

"I thought you were telling a true story," she said.

Grandpa Allen sighed. "I know this is hard to believe. If I had not lived it myself, I would not believe it either."

"Are you saying it was a magic cave?" asked Morgan.

"All I can tell you is that the combination of placed stones and the string of sounds, 'Ah Bah Say Sum', opened the secret cave, not just for the leader, but for me as well," replied Grandpa Allen.

There was an awkward silence in the room as Grandpa Allen waited for Morgan's reaction.

Rusty reached down and petted Jip, who had laid his head on Rusty's knee. "I didn't believe him either the first time he told me," confessed Rusty. "I thought he was trying to play a joke on me. But after you see what we have to show you—just— you'll see, I promise."

"Show me what?" asked Morgan.

"We are getting ahead of ourselves," said Grandpa Allen. He took a sip of his tea and continued his story.

"After carrying my master's goods inside the cave, the leader took the stones from their nooks, hid them, and repeated the magic word. The cave closed, and the thieves left, disappearing into the woods. I sat on my boulder for a long while waiting. Finally, I was shivering so much from the cold that I had to start moving. Climbing down, I crept to the cliff face."

Grandpa Allen leaned over and reached into a drawer of the side table near him. He took out a sheaf of papers that were yellow with age. Sorting through them, he handed Morgan and Rusty a drawing. Morgan peered closely at a crude pencil sketch of images.

"When I stood where the leader of thieves stood facing the cliff, I found the pattern of images you see drawn on the top portion of the page," explained Grandpa Allen.

"The empty boxes represent the nooks where I had seen him place the stones he kept hidden. I searched behind the nearby boulder and found the bag of individual stones pretty quickly. I've drawn the images that were on those stones on the bottom portion of the page."

"Each image on the bottom portion of the page fits into an empty box on the top portion, creating a pattern."

Grandpa Allen waited while Morgan examined the sheet. She could see that there was a pattern to the lines of carved images on the top. There was a simple outline of a figure with a lightning bolt across it. There was a drawing of what looked to be a cloud. Morgan pointed at various carved images of the individual stones from the bottom of the page then slid her finger up to show Rusty where she thought they could be placed in the empty boxes at the top of the page, among the pattern found on the cliff face. Rusty smiled and nodded, then looked up at Grandpa Allen.

"She got it," he said.

Grandpa handed over a sheet that contained the cliff images put together with the separate stone images.

"But what does it mean?" asked Morgan.

Grandpa Allen shrugged. "We don't know. The images look similar to petroglyph rock carvings. A friend who studies the

Algonquin, people who've lived in this region for over ten thousand years, tried to find out what the images mean. But no group has claimed the carvings as their own, and no one has been able to translate them. The Algonquin do know of the cave site, and they say the thieves took over the area years ago. Everything about the cave remains a mystery.

"But back to my story," said Grandpa Allen. "I placed the stones in their proper nook and stood before the cliff face. 'Ah Bah Say Sum,' I shouted, and to my amazement, the cave opened. I saw the sacks with my master's goods just inside, so I carried them to my sturdy pony and put them together into larger sacks, and tied them on top of the saddle.

"I went back to the cave to explore and found a deeper cavern filled with riches! There were gold and silver coins, silverware, and jewelry."

Morgan gasped, "What did you do?"

"I was speechless with excitement and felt like the luckiest lad alive," smiled Grandpa Allen. "I remember running my fingers through piles of coins, stuffing them into my pockets, dancing around with such abandon that I slipped and fell on the rocky floor. That brought me back to my senses. I needed my hands free to lead my horse down the hill, so I found a saddlebag that I could put around my neck. I stuffed the bag with necklaces and more coins. I wasn't sure if it was right to steal from thieves, but being a poor lad, it proved too tempting for me.

"I went through the ritual of taking out the stones and saying Ah Bah Say Sum, and the cave closed. Then I made the long journey home on foot, leading the small horse."

"Your master must have been pleased with you," said Morgan.

"He was," agreed Grandpa Allen. "He even gave me the gift of the Welsh pony for my efforts. I would have been content, had it not been for my older brother. Even though I shared with him my secret stash in the saddlebag and my pockets, my brother told me I was a fool. He was very angry with me. He said I shouldn't have bothered with the master's goods, but taken large sacks for the two of us, so that we could be rich for the rest of our lives. I could see his point, but I was happy that I had retrieved what was stolen. The master had always been good to me. He had taken us in when our parents both died of whooping cough. We were only six and ten at the time, and he'd been kind to us for the most part."

Grandpa Allen paused and reached over to take a sip of his tea. Morgan could see the sorrow he still felt at losing both his parents. She shuddered thinking about it. Just knowing her father was lost was almost more than she could bear. Grandpa Allen continued.

"My brother yelled at me over the next few days until I finally agreed that I would return with him to the cave. I had told no one but my brother about the cave, so it was our secret. He made me draw a map, and the images on the cliff face, so I wouldn't forget anything. We made plans to sneak away one night with my new horse and some sacks to carry more riches. My brother told me to go to sleep and assured me he would wake me when it was time to go. I slept and woke up when it was nearly dawn. My brother was nowhere to be found, and my little pony was gone too."

"Oh No!" exclaimed Morgan.

"I didn't know what to think, and I was worried about him. I left before everyone awoke and made the long trek to the cave. There I found my pony sitting outside, but I couldn't find my brother. There were large sacks stuffed with treasure loaded on my pony's back, and he had been left tied next to the entrance. I started to take the sacks off to ride fast for help, but I stopped. What would my brother say? He would be so angry with me if I left the sacks. Even though I spent hours looking for him, I found no signs of him anywhere near the cave. So, in the end, I walked my Welsh pony all the way home, arriving just after nightfall.

"Leading my pony to the back pasture, I hid him behind some trees. Then I started back inside to tell my master and the household what had happened. As I was crossing a field in back of the property, I saw a huge group of men sneaking through the tall grass in front of me. Immediately I hid in the trees, and, sure enough, when they came close, I could see the leader of the thieves with his shiny bald head. He motioned for his men to go in different directions to search for me. They hadn't seen me yet, so I crept back to my pony and escaped.

"After all these years, I've thought so often about the choices I made. I searched endlessly for my brother, hoping he had escaped the clutches of the thieves. Finally, I decided to travel far enough to be safe, but close enough that I could continue the search for my brother."

Grandpa Allen looked very sad. He paused and rubbed his eyes wearily.

Morgan hesitated. "But you never found him."

"No," said Grandpa Allen, "I never saw him again."

He put his teacup on the tray and stood up slowly. Morgan was at a loss for words. She felt how hard it must have been for Grandpa Allen to lose everyone he loved.

"There is more to the story," said Grandpa Allen, "but it is growing late, and I think it best that we begin again tomorrow."

Morgan stood, and Jip jumped up happily on her knees. Stroking Jip, she said, "Thank you for the story. I'll be very excited to listen to you again tomorrow."

Grandpa Allen chuckled, and Rusty smiled with him.

"We won't be telling you much tomorrow, my dear. No— most of the story is done. And I have saved the best for last. Remember, I said that we wanted to share with you our greatest secret?"

Morgan nodded.

Grandpa Allen smiled. "Well, tomorrow, we will *show* you!"

Chapter Seven

THE GREAT SECRET

"We never know how high we are
Till we are called to rise. . ."

Emily Dickinson

MORGAN felt something furry hit her, and she woke up. Jip's head was lying against hers on the pillow. Morgan sat up, rubbing her forehead, and looked around her bare room. Just a day had passed, and so much had changed—only now Morgan didn't mind. It was all so exciting. Today she would find out the great secret!

When Morgan arrived upstairs, she discovered that Grandpa Allen and Rusty had already eaten.

"C'mon slowpoke," Rusty called to her as he and Grandpa Allen were walking out the back door.

But Dara wouldn't let her leave without a proper meal. Grumbling, Morgan sat down in the kitchen to eat poached eggs with asparagus tips and toast. Miss Stern walked in, jingling a set of keys. She eyed Morgan suspiciously, but Morgan kept her eyes down. She had not spoken to Miss Stern yet, and she wanted to keep it that way. Finishing her meal, Morgan gulped down some water and jumped up to run outside. Jip darted up too and followed at her heels.

Grandpa Allen and Rusty were waiting for her in the garden.

"Will you show me the secret now?" Morgan asked, panting as she ran up to them.

Grandpa Allen quickly looked to see if anyone was near them. "Discretion child," he said.

"What does that mean?" Morgan asked.

"You'll get used to it," Rusty told her. "I usually don't understand half of what he says. Right now, he means that we have to be careful, so no one else finds out our secret."

"Let us start where we lost the trail of the thieves yesterday," said Grandpa Allen. "Even if we only pick up a few clues, it might be helpful."

Morgan walked through the morning woods. The leaves were the light green of early summer, and the air still held the scent of dew. Grandpa Allen and Rusty were just ahead in a clearing, and she saw Rusty stop and look around. He seemed confused.

"Maybe that way." Rusty pointed north.

They suddenly saw a figure through the trees running away from them.

"Could that be one of them?" shouted Morgan. "Why would they be back here?"

"Because they didn't get what they wanted," shouted Grandpa Allen. "Go, Rusty!"

Morgan watched as Rusty leaped to run after the man, and in mid-air, there was a dazzling flash of light, so fast and harsh that it left her blinking. Dots of brightness swam before her eyes as if scorched into her vision. Following the light, was a deep drumroll of thunder. It started with a loud boom and then rolled over her with the force of a fierce wave at sea. Amid this burst of energy, the light swallowed Rusty, and finishing the leap out the other side was a gigantic wolf—the same one she had seen twice before. Morgan stood in place, shocked into stillness, her mouth hanging open. Thoughts sped past in her mind.

How did that happen? she wondered. *It can't be. It's just not possible.*

Grandpa Allen began moving quickly after the thief and the wolf. "Come, child. We must not let them get too far ahead," he urged.

Morgan shook off her shock and began to run after Grandpa Allen. They were racing past trees that slapped them with their branches and leaping over logs and low shrubs in their path when they heard a fierce howl that was abruptly cut off. Grandpa Allen looked concerned.

"Rusty?" he shouted. "Rusty, are you okay?"

There was only an answering whine—this time much softer. Morgan ran past Grandpa Allen toward the sound, barely managing to stop herself from falling into a large hole in the ground. Looking over the edge, she saw the massive wolf in the hole.

Can he jump out? How far down there is he? she wondered.

Morgan quickly tried to estimate the depth of the hole. She had stood next to the wolf the day before, and she knew it was about three feet tall. She guessed that about five wolves, standing on one another's shoulders, could reach the top.

Can you estimate how deep the hole is?

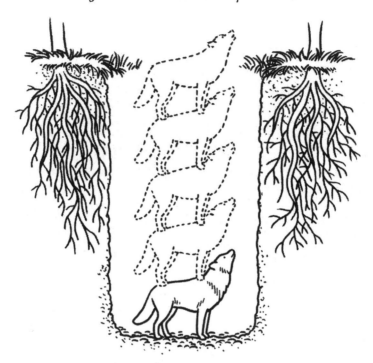

I could count by threes, five times on my fingers, Morgan thought.

3, 6, 9, 12, 15

Or I could add three together five times.

$$3 + 3 + 3 + 3 + 3 = 15$$

Or I could also multiply 3 x 5 = 15.

Fifteen feet is too deep for the wolf to jump! she realized.

Indeed, as she watched the wolf pace back and forth, she saw that there wasn't even enough room at the bottom for him to get a running leap to scramble up the sides. Although the wolf tried, again and again, he kept falling back down to the bottom. The walls were too steep for a four-legged creature to climb.

Grandpa Allen joined Morgan at the edge of the hole. Morgan noticed woven sticks at the bottom broken into pieces, and scattered among the sticks was a large pile of dead forest leaves. She imagined in her mind the woven sticks placed over the hole with the leaves on top. The wolf would have never noticed any difference on the ground when he was running after the thief.

"I think it was a trap," she said.

Grandpa Allen nodded. "They must have seen the wolf following them yesterday, and they knew we'd be back, so they worked last night to set this up. The hole was probably already here. They may have made it a bit deeper, then hid it from sight." He called down to the wolf, "Rusty, are you okay?"

The wolf sat back and snarled at him. Then to Morgan's shock, there was another flash of light with a rumble of thunder, and the wolf changed back into the curly redhead she knew. Rusty was rubbing one of his legs, and he was filthy from head to toe.

"I'll live. My leg hurts a little," Rusty said. "They set that trap for me. I was lucky I didn't break my neck!"

"I'm sure that is what they hoped for—otherwise, they never would have worked this hard," agreed Grandpa Allen. "I'm sorry, my boy, I believe this trap was laid for me. If nothing else, it is a rather sinister warning."

Morgan was still trying to process the fact that Rusty had changed to a wolf and back again.

Rusty looked at Morgan's confused face and suddenly grinned. "Woof!" he said.

Morgan stood there, not knowing what to say.

"I know it's a lot to take in," Grandpa Allen said gently.

Morgan still said nothing. She had such a jumble of thoughts going around in her head.

Grandpa Allen called down to Rusty. "I'll get you out of there, but we must not let the thief get away. Can you throw it up to me?"

Rusty stood and took the medallion off from around his neck. It took a couple of tries, but finally, he managed to toss it over the upper edge of the hole. Grandpa Allen picked it up and handed it to Morgan. She turned it over in her hands, examining it. She felt this strange feeling—like she didn't want to let it go.

I like the feel of it, she thought.

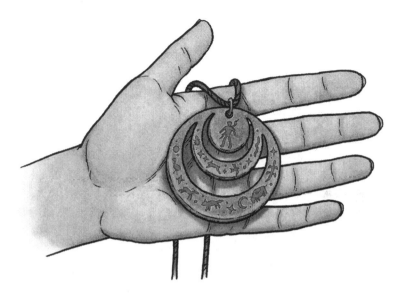

"Amazing, huh? Look at all the animals," called Rusty. Morgan looked over the edge at him. He seemed a long way down, and so much smaller and more vulnerable when he wasn't in his wolf shape.

Grandpa Allen pointed to the medallion. "In the center, you will see there is the image of a lightning man."

"The same symbol that was part of the carving on the cliff face where you found the cave," said Morgan.

"Exactly. We do not know how it works, but we do know that it is an object of power. You've seen how it can transform living beings. I know that today there are scientists who theorize that the first signs of life could have been sparked by lightning," Grandpa Allen said, "but I do not pretend to understand any of this really."

Morgan looked at him. "*This* is what the thieves were looking for? I thought it might be the blue gem necklace you were carrying the other day."

"Ah. So, you caught that. I shouldn't be surprised," said Grandpa Allen. "No. I guard that necklace safely for other reasons. It belonged to my dear wife, Isabelle, who passed away some years ago."

"Oh," said Morgan, "I'm sorry." She didn't know what else to say.

"That's alright, my dear. When you get to be my age, you've lost so many people close to your heart. You learn to delight even more in those that remain." He smiled at her fondly. Morgan felt the kindness of his warm gaze. She glanced down at the medallion then looked at it more closely.

"What do the stars mean?"

Grandpa Allen seemed distracted. "What? Oh." He paused for a moment. "Such a simple question which never occurred to me. When I think about it, the answer might not be so simple."

He seemed caught in a reverie, but then he turned to look in the direction the thief had disappeared. "At the moment, we need to focus. If we can catch up to that thief, he could lead us to where the others are hiding out. Then we can make plans to protect ourselves and the medallion. Its power is too great to let it fall into the wrong hands."

"But how can we catch up with him?" she asked. "He must be a mile away by now."

"Not we," Grandpa Allen said, "You. Unfortunately, I am too old to use the powers. They take energy that I simply do not have anymore. And I need to stay here and get poor Rusty out of this trap. I was hoping—I know it's a great deal to ask, but we have so little time to decide—if you could put it on. If you could change into something capable of catching up to the thief." He stopped, hesitating. "I'm afraid it's our only hope right now."

Morgan stood quietly, holding the medallion in her hands. She looked down at Rusty and then up at Grandpa Allen.

"Don't worry, Morgan. It doesn't hurt or anything," Rusty promised. "I've only ever been able to turn into a wolf, which was the first animal I thought of, so be careful about which animal you choose."

"After many years of using it, I could change into just about any animal I wanted," Grandpa Allen told her. "It is true, however, that you must pick wisely this first time as it can take much practice to be able to choose other animals."

Feeling afraid and excited at the same time, Morgan placed the medallion around her neck. It tingled on her skin, and she suddenly felt a burst of energy, like she could do anything.

She closed her eyes to quiet her mind. Breathing in and out slowly, she watched her breath, letting her thoughts go, and filling herself with air and space. She could feel the tingling sensation of the medallion growing stronger. Then she focused very carefully on the animal she wanted to be.

As Morgan stood still with her eyes closed, Grandpa Allen tried to assure her. "It can take a while to—" but he suddenly laughed out loud. At the same moment, she realized that the tingling in her chest was spreading over her entire body. There was a flash and then a rumble of thunder. She looked up, and Grandpa Allen seemed to rise over her. She saw every detail in his amazed expression.

Without pausing, she turned and leaped into the air, then flapped hard with her giant wings.

Rusty let out a whoop!

Morgan shot up through the trees, up and up toward the high clouds. She felt the wind through her feathers and a lightness of heart she never imagined possible.

She had done it. She had changed. And now she was flying!

Chapter Eight

THE SHAPE OF THINGS

*"The power of the world
always works in circles,
and everything tries to be round."*

Black Elk

MORGAN felt the lift of warm air under her wings, and she let it propel her higher into the clouds. Swooping below for a better look, she saw the tops of the trees stretching on for miles.

I can't believe I'm flying! she thought.

Then she remembered why she was here in the first place. With her new keen eyesight, she scanned the tracks between the trees.

How easy it is to see all the details with the eyes of an eagle! she realized.

For that is what she had become. A graceful golden eagle, just like the pictures her father had shown her when he told her why he had decided to become a mapmaker.

He was right, she thought. *It is calm and peaceful up here in the clouds. I wish he could be here with me right now!*

Suddenly she saw someone running at the edge of the forest where the trees turned into open pasture. It was the thief, the one that had lured Rusty into the trap.

Got you! she thought.

Observing the thief from high up, she tried to note details about him. He was wearing a dark felt hat with a short brim, and a black vest without a shirt, leaving his arms bare. Every once in a while, as he ran, he would yank up his pants or clamp a hand on his hat, making his gait awkward and clumsy.

Morgan followed the thief for a very long way. Now that she had him in her sights, she relaxed and enjoyed the feeling of being so high and being able to see the earth laid out below her like a vast living map. She looked in the distance and saw the whole round world stretched before her—as if it went on forever. Morgan thought about how, if she flew straight for months, she would return to this same place.

She could see rivers wind their way down from higher hills into the valleys, and off to her right was the sweeping expanse of a sparkling ocean. Beneath her, the forest gave way to farms and then to clusters of houses and stores that made up the small town of Harlow, a place where Morgan and her mother had stopped on the way to Rusty's home. Along the river north of town, she could see the thief moving swiftly into another immense forest. She stayed above him as he followed the river, catching sight of him from time to time as she drifted overhead.

Then in the distance, she saw a big clearing in the woods. The river ran along one side. Morgan saw a large fenced area that looked as if it had been a corral long ago, and the ruins of an old cabin with the roof collapsed, and only the chimney left standing. Dotted throughout the abandoned corral were many rectangular structures. She saw some men cooking at a campfire, and others gathered in a circle, playing a card game.

The man she had been tracking trotted into the clearing and then headed for a large rectangle that was off to one side on its own.

I've done it, she thought. *I've found where the thieves are hiding out. This is their camp!*

Part of her wanted to fly straight back to Grandpa Allen and Rusty and tell them what she had found. She realized, though, that this was the perfect time for her to gather information on these dangerous men.

Morgan's View of the Thief Camp

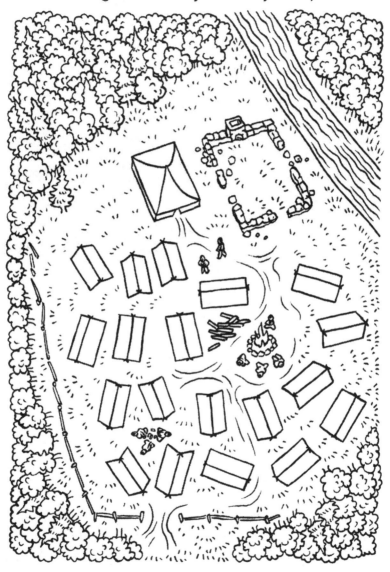

Circling above the camp, Morgan took in everything that she saw. She started to count the men, but some disappeared under the structures while others came out, and she realized just counting would never work. Then she thought of an easier way to figure out how many men there were.

Diving close to the ground, she saw that the rectangles dotted throughout the corral became more like triangles as she got lower.

Tent from directly above   *Tent from lower angle*

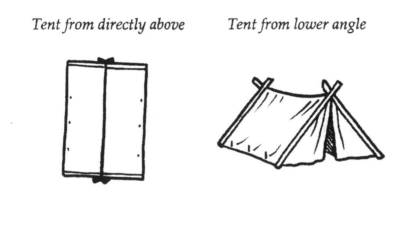

The structures were simple canvas fabric draped across crossed poles with a rope tied between the poles to make tents.

I can figure out how many men sleep in each tent and then count the tents, she thought.

As she passed over a tent, she estimated how long and wide it was. They were little more than the length of a man, and it looked like two men lying side by side could fit under each tent. Then she rose again and counted the smaller tents from above.

Can you estimate the number of thieves?

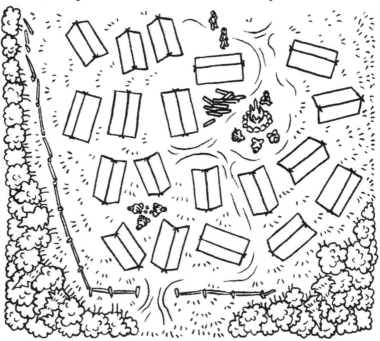

She counted nineteen small tents, with two men in each.

I could count by twos up to nineteen fingers—if I still had fingers! she thought.

Or I could add nineteen to itself, or multiply nineteen times two.

19 + 19 = 38 or 19 x 2 = 38

So, there were about thirty-eight men, plus the people in the bigger tent near the ruins of the old cabin. That made about forty men in all. She swooped down to get a better look at the big tent, and a large, bald figure emerged. He was quite old looking, but he still seemed strong. He was yanking at the thief that she had been following. Pulling the man out of the tent, the bald guy shook him, threw him to the ground and began yelling at him.

Morgan wasn't near enough to hear what the bald leader was saying, but she was frightened of him and didn't want to get any closer. Then the man's sharp eyes caught sight of her, and he stopped, staring straight at her. She felt nervous, so she flew up and away from him. Looking back toward the ground, she could still see the leader with his head tilted back, shading his eyes as he tried to track her in the sky.

He ran back into the tent, and Morgan felt relieved, but then she saw he was coming back out carrying a rifle. He searched the sky, and Morgan realized what he was about to do. She flapped her wings as hard as she could, racing to get away. Behind her, she heard the loud BOOM of the gun.

Chapter Nine

TAKEN

*"Do not worry about your
difficulties in mathematics.
I assure you that mine are greater."*

Albert Einstein

IN the mid-day sun, Morgan circled over the mansion that still didn't feel like home. Although, as she thought about it, she realized that Rusty and Grandpa Allen had come a long way in a short time to feel like family.

She scanned the grounds carefully to make sure that when she landed, no one would see her. She was lucky to have escaped the thief camp without being shot. On the return trip, she still marveled at the view laid out below her, but her wings had started to ache. She understood what Grandpa Allen meant when he said changing into an animal took so much energy. Now that she was home, she felt very tired and hungry.

Her eagle eyes caught the tiny form of a field mouse, and her animal instincts kicked in. She was just about to dive for her prey when she stopped herself, remembering that she could land, change back, and walk into the house for the mid-day meal.

Morgan spied a space between the garden and the stables that looked deserted. Quickly tucking her wings to her sides, she dove straight down and landed smoothly. She loved the feeling of being an eagle—it seemed to come so naturally.

As she transformed back, her body crackled with the same flash of light and shook with a rumble of thunder. Resting a moment, she looked down and saw that she was indeed herself again, with the medallion hanging around her neck. She tucked the medallion away inside her dress and started for the house.

As she rounded a hedge toward the garden, Rusty came running out to greet her.

"I listened for the thunder and followed the sound," he said to her breathlessly. "How was it? What did you find?"

"I found the thief camp!" Morgan told him proudly.

"That's great!" Rusty exclaimed, "Let's go tell Grandpa Allen."

"Can we eat first?" pleaded Morgan. "I'm starving!"

"Oh, of course. I forgot. It does knock the stuff out of you, doesn't it? And you were an eagle—that's fantastic! What was it like flying? I'm a bit jealous, actually. I don't think I could become a bird or any other animal for a while yet. I've tried. How incredible to be able to fly!"

Rusty rambled on as they returned to the house, and Morgan just listened. She would have answered him if she could, but at this point, it felt like she might fall asleep while walking. She trudged on, unable to think of anything but food and bed.

⋙⋘

Morgan awoke to her little bare room, with Jip lying beside her and her mother stroking her hair.

"How are you, my sweet? Are you ill?" her mother asked with concern.

Morgan was so groggy and confused that she thought for a moment she might have been dreaming. Secretively, she felt for the medallion, and it was still there, tingling on her skin. She dared not take it out. She had promised to keep it a secret.

"I'm fine, mother," she managed to say sleepily. "How did I get here?"

"Well, you fell asleep at the table." Morgan's mother smiled. She looked relieved that Morgan wasn't sick.

"Rusty was down here waiting for you to wake up for the longest time. I finally told him to go and do something useful.

He said he'd be in the stables." Morgan's mother paused and looked at her knowingly. "He was very anxious to talk to you. Is something going on that I should know, Morgiana?"

Morgan turned to pet Jip, fearing her mother would see the truth in her eyes. She felt bad, not telling her—they usually shared everything—but she had promised.

"I'm just getting used to things being so new and different," Morgan said cautiously. That was true, but it wasn't the whole truth by half. Morgan didn't know what to do.

Her mother waited patiently, but when Morgan said nothing more, she sighed. "Well I have to admit I've been a bit anxious about the thieves breaking in, and you all were gone so long this morning, and then when Rusty and Grandpa Allen returned and you weren't with them. . . then you showed up so tired you could barely eat."

Morgan's mother paused.

Morgan sat up and hugged her mother. "Don't worry. I'll be fine," she assured her.

Morgan's mother hesitated. That's when Morgan noticed that she held a crumpled piece of paper in her hand. Dara saw Morgan looking at the paper, and she unfolded it, smoothing it out on the surface of the bed.

"It's a telegram sent to Grandpa Allen," she said, showing it to Morgan. "It's from the **Department of Zoology at Stanford University**. They are the ones heading the expedition to the Galapagos. They've had word of some survivors from a storm at sea. They washed up on one of the islands where there is a sugar cane factory."

Morgan felt her chest tighten with nerves as she took the paper from her mother's hands and read the bold type of the telegram.

Western United Telegram Company

CABLE SERVICE ACROSS THE GLOBE.
HIRAM WADE, PRESIDENT AND GENERAL MANAGER

RECEIVED at   BOSTON MASS.   1899

12 Shipwrecked survivorsfound near Chatham Island
Plantation.Good possibility they are from the
Hopkins-Stanford GalapagosExpedition. No word of
identities yet. Will keep you informed as news arrives.
Robert E. Snodgrass
Professor, Departmentof Zoology
Stanford University

Morgan's breath caught. She could scarcely believe that after all this time, they finally had some word. She looked at her mother to find Dara's eyes glistening with tears.

"There's hope!" her mother said fiercely.

"Let it be him," Morgan replied. Then thinking of Rusty, "And Rusty's father too," she added.

"Yes, both of them." Dara agreed as she leaned forward and held Morgan tight.

After a moment, Morgan leaned back. "Does Rusty know?"

"Grandpa Allen showed him the telegram at lunch," her mother assured her.

Morgan brushed down her wrinkled frock as she stood up off the bed. "I should go find Rusty."

⤜⋙⋘⤛

Morgan felt blinded in the dark of the stables as she stepped inside. When her eyes adjusted, she saw Rusty a few stalls away, brushing down a golden-colored foal with a large white patch on his forehead. The little foal turned to nip Rusty on his arm, and she laughed.

Rusty turned at the sound of her laughter. "You're awake, finally!"

Morgan smiled excitedly. "The telegram!"

Rusty grinned. "Best news yet. Nothing for certain, of course, but. . ."

"*Good possibility*, the telegram said. I don't think they'd give us that hope if they didn't mean it," Morgan said as she leaned on the foal's stall.

"I know, right?" Rusty agreed. "I'm almost afraid to think about it too much—like I could jinx it or something." He turned and continued brushing down the foal, and Morgan decided she should change the subject.

"How long did I sleep?" she asked.

"Hours!" Rusty complained as he set the brush aside. "You fell asleep in your soup," he teased. "Grandpa Allen went to sleep after the meal as well. It took a lot out of him to get me out of that trap."

"Oh, the trap!" Morgan exclaimed. "How *did* you get out?"

"Grandpa figured it out. He broke off a bunch of small tree limbs and managed to hold them together with his belt and necktie. He even somehow wound his vest and coat at the base to make the whole thing more stable. It took a lot of tries, but I finally made it up," Rusty explained.

"Can I pet him?" Morgan asked, glancing at the foal.

"Sure, come on in," he said, opening the gate to the foal's stall. Morgan stepped inside and stroked the foal's neck. Reaching to touch the mark on the young horse's face, she felt the *huff* of his warm breath.

"What's his name?" she asked.

"Patch," replied Rusty, and Morgan laughed. "That's perfect," she said. "I used to have a pony named Bailey. I really, really miss her."

"Well, you can come and play with Patch anytime," Rusty assured her.

Watching Rusty as he moved to put away his tools, Morgan thought about how neither of them had brothers or sisters. She didn't know what it was like to have a big brother, but as she stood there, she realized that she'd want him to be just like Rusty.

Wiping his hands on his pants, Rusty said, "I want to hear your story, but we should go find Grandpa Allen, so you don't have to tell the whole thing twice."

"Good idea. I'm still so tired," Morgan complained.

"Yeah. I always feel like I've been through the wringer," Rusty agreed. "That's why Grandpa Allen can't do it anymore."

They left the stable and started toward the house. As they rounded the hedge to the gardens, Morgan asked, "So how did Grandpa Allen first find the medallion?"

Rusty stopped and turned to her. "I didn't want to disturb you while you slept, but—may I see it?"

She pulled it out from under her collar and showed it to him. "Do you want it back?" she asked.

He seemed to relax a bit. "You can keep it for now. I just wanted to be sure it was safe."

She could feel his reluctance. "It has a certain pull, doesn't it?" she asked.

"Yes. That's why Grandpa Allen first put it on. I guess there is something about its power that makes you want to have it near. He found it in the saddlebag he'd taken from the cave. He wore it around so much he forgot he even had it on sometimes."

"What did Grandpa Allen turn into first?" Morgan asked as they entered the house.

Rusty laughed. "A mouse! He was caught hiding in a stable when the thieves were chasing him in a little town about fifty miles north. The thieves were searching the stable, and their leader walked in. Grandpa thought for sure he was done for. He wished he were a mouse so that he could crawl right past them, and *Poof!*"

As they started up the stairway, Rusty continued. "Unfortunately, the leader of the thieves saw the change happen, or at least he saw Grandpa Allen disappear in a flash. It was years later when Grandfather Allen figured out that the saddlebag that he'd taken from the secret cave belonged to the leader of the thieves."

"So, the leader already knew about the medallion and its powers," said Morgan.

Rusty shrugged, "We're not sure. All we know is that he never forgot, and after all these years, he's still after Grandpa."

Morgan thought to herself and smiled. "A mouse. That must have been a shock."

They had reached the long hallway leading to the beautiful bedroom and started down it.

Rusty chuckled. "All Grandpa knew was the flash and rumble, and then suddenly he was on the floor, and everything around him had grown huge!" Rusty gestured grandly with his arms. "He ran and hid in a hole."

The children laughed together as Rusty opened the bedroom door. They stepped inside and saw the room was in shambles.

Morgan gasped, "Not again!"

"These guys have no imagination," Rusty agreed. Nervously he called out, "Grandpa?"

Morgan joined him, looking around. "Grandpa Allen?" she called.

There was no answer.

Morgan pointed to a teacup lying on the carpet, with a splatter of dark stains around it. Rusty turned and ran over to the vanity table, and Morgan saw that it was pushed aside, and the mirror was partially open. Rusty yanked it open the rest of the way, and they both saw that the secret door behind was wide open, showing the dark tunnel beyond.

He turned to Morgan in a panic. "They've got him! The thieves took Grandpa Allen!"

Chapter Ten

THE SEARCH

*"It's not that I'm so smart.
It's just that I spent more
time on problems."*

Albert Einstein

Mr. Grennan walked into the bedroom to collect the remains of the afternoon tea. He paused when he saw the state of the room and the children.

"What're you two about now?" he asked.

Rusty eased the mirror closed as he spoke. "Mr. Grennan, the thieves have taken Grandpa Allen. You've got to get everyone together to search for him! You can start at the old spring, and follow their trail."

Morgan cut in. "If the trail becomes confusing, go toward the town of Harlow and then keep heading north along the river.

There's a clearing next to the river about five miles into the woods."

"And just how would you be knowin' that?" asked Mr. Grennan doubtfully.

"I'm sorry, but there's no time," explained Rusty. "You must gather everyone now." "Please!" Rusty added when the butler hesitated.

Mr. Grennan shook his head and hurried off.

Rusty turned to Morgan when he was gone. "The thieves have probably already made it to the old spring."

"If only we could both change! I should give this back." She lifted the medallion from around her neck.

"No need, Morgan." He opened his shirt to show her the three white circles on his chest. "As long as these marks remain, the powers remain with us. It usually takes a couple of days for them to go away."

Morgan lifted the medallion, from beneath her collar. Underneath on her skin were three perfect circles of white. She brushed them with her fingertips. "So that's what the marks mean. I wondered. There's been so much excitement I forgot to ask."

Rusty and Morgan moved quickly out to the hallway.

"So, the thieves are holed up about five miles north of Harlow?" he asked.

"Yes. Along the river," said Morgan. "How far is Harlow from here?"

"About four or five miles north," said Rusty.

"So, five miles to Harlow plus five miles to the camp means they're about ten miles from here. An eagle can fly about thirty miles an hour over long distances," Morgan told him.

"How do you know that?" asked Rusty.

"My father loves eagles. That's how I thought to become one," Morgan explained.

"Well, still. I don't want you to fly ahead. Let's stick together," said Rusty. "It's too dangerous. As a wolf, I can sprint almost that fast, but only for a short way."

As the children came down the stairway, they could see that the household was in an uproar. Mr. Grennan was shouting orders to everyone, and maids were running to and fro gathering blankets, water, and coats, while a burly, gray-haired man was grabbing rifles from a gun case.

The children saw Dara enter the front hall, and, without saying a word to each other, they ducked behind the stairway. They knew they would have to skirt around the mad rush of adults, or they would be forced to stay home.

Rusty motioned to a side hall, and he and Morgan snuck out of the front entryway. They were halfway down the hall when they heard the familiar, heavy click-clack of heels nearing them from the other end. Rusty quickly opened a nearby door, and he and Morgan stepped inside a musty closet, waiting for the unfriendly Miss Stern to pass.

"Could you figure out how many thieves there were?" Rusty whispered.

"I think maybe around forty," Morgan whispered back. She was grateful she had thought to figure that out when she was back at their camp. Miss Stern's heavy stomping faded, and Rusty stepped back out into the passageway.

"How many searchers will there be?" Morgan asked.

"I think only about ten," said Rusty.

How many thieves are there compared to how many rescuers?

"That's not very good odds," said Morgan.

"Forty thieves to ten rescuers is four to one, or four thieves against each rescuer," observed Rusty grimly. "But we might catch up to them before they reach their camp," he said.

The children had arrived outside, and they ran toward a large garden hedge.

"Should we follow the rescuers?" asked Morgan breathlessly as they ran.

"They'll be too slow!" exclaimed Rusty. "Did you hear? They're getting a wagon ready. Probably because Grandpa Allen can't ride a horse very far anymore."

"How fast can you go then?" asked Morgan. "Maybe. . . ten miles an hour," estimated Rusty.

The children ran behind the hedge to a secluded spot. Rusty glanced around to make sure no one could see them.

"So, if the camp is ten miles away and that takes you an hour to run, then it will be about an hour until we can get to Grandpa Allen," she calculated.

"But hopefully they won't yet be at the camp once we catch up to them so that will be even less time," he said again.

"Hopefully," she agreed. "What are we going to do when we catch up with them anyway?" she asked.

"We'll think of something," Rusty said with confidence.

But Morgan wasn't so sure. "Okay. You just run, and I'll keep track of you," she said.

There was a flash and then a rumble of thunder, and Morgan flew up, not bothering to wait for Rusty. By the time she did look down, she could see the wolf below her, racing through the woods toward the old spring.

Circling the mansion, she watched as tiny figures below drove a wagon to the front door. Then curving in the direction Rusty had gone, she flapped her wings hard and sped north.

As she flew, a bank of puffy clouds appeared, and then engulfed her. Sounds dropped away as the cloud mist grew thick, and water droplets gathered along her wings. Despite her fear for Grandpa Allen, she began to feel more relaxed, like she was in a safe cocoon of white. Suddenly, she burst out of the clouds into the afternoon sun and felt the deep delight of being able to fly. She checked below for Rusty and caught sight of him as he loped by the old spring.

The pace was slow and easy for her, which gave her time to think. Although Morgan hoped they soon caught up with the thieves, she figured enough time had passed for the thieves to make it back to their camp; she should prepare for the worst. She tried out all kinds of different scenarios in her mind—ways that she and Rusty could manage to help Grandpa Allen escape.

By the time she and Rusty reached the town of Harlow, there was still no sign of the thieves. But that was okay because her ideas were coming together in rich detail.

She had a plan.

Chapter Eleven

THE ESCAPE ATTEMPT

"Hope is the thing with feathers
That perches in the soul,
And sings the tune without the words,
And never stops at all. . ."

Emily Dickinson

MORGAN walked into the camp of thieves on her own two legs with her heart thumping wildly, and her throat so tight she could barely breathe. Making the plan was one thing, but carrying it out was proving much harder.

Now that she was in among the makeshift tents, she could smell the stench of sweat mingled with campfire smoke. Peeking around a canvas, she glimpsed a group of thieves working over a cooking pot. There were three of them all wearing suspenders holding up ill-fitting pants. One of them was barefoot, and he coughed and spat into the fire, making a sizzling sound.

Though she hid, the whole point was for her to be seen, but not too soon. Not before she found Grandpa Allen and the leader of the thieves.

And that was the main reason for her fear. Just this morning, the leader had taken out his rifle and tried to shoot her down. She hadn't told Rusty that part. He wouldn't have let her try this scheme if she had.

Morgan ducked low as two thieves who were arguing walked by. Waiting until they passed, she crawled on her hands and knees until she could see the larger tent off to one side, near the rubble of the cabin. There was a lot of space between where she knelt and the large tent where she wanted to be. Morgan couldn't figure out how to get across without being seen. She could change into a smaller animal, but she was going to need every bit of energy she had in just a moment, so Morgan stayed where she was, looking for a safe opening.

Something moved in the shadows near the cabin. Morgan saw Rusty in his wolf form streak silently through the ruins, and then disappear behind the standing chimney. She and Rusty had argued about who was going to do what in her plan. She had finally demonstrated what she could do, and in the end, he had reluctantly admitted that her way was the only one that would work.

Right now, Morgan would have been happy to be anywhere else. She was more frightened than she'd ever been. Slipping inside a tent, she took a moment to calm down. Doubts kept creeping into her mind, but she tried to let them go. She closed her eyes in the way she had practiced so often. She concentrated on her breath, and eventually, her body settled, and she could feel her heart beat more slowly. Everything depended on her ability to think and act quickly, and she couldn't do that if she were in a panic.

Sticking her head out, she was planning to sneak across to the big tent, when the flap jerked open, and the large, bald-headed leader emerged. He was far more striking than the other men, and also far better dressed in a jacket and wool trousers that looked as if they'd been custom-made to fit his big frame. Behind him in the shadow, Morgan caught sight of a pair of bound feet. Morgan made a quick decision and stood. She walked out to the center of the open space, facing the bald leader.

"I know you have someone tied up inside your tent!" she shouted at him. Just beyond the bald man, the wolf's head jerked up at her words, so she knew Rusty had heard.

The bald man laughed, unconcerned. "And just who are you?" he asked, his voice more polished than she'd expected.

Morgan reached inside her shift and pulled out the medallion for the leader to see clearly. "I'm the person who has what you want." With a flash and a rumble—she vanished.

The leader shouted, "Get her, you idiots!" He pointed to a space where nothing but air remained. His men began to run toward where he pointed, but the man at the front of the pack abruptly stopped when he couldn't see what he was supposed to be chasing, and the thief behind collided into him.

Meanwhile, Morgan lay quietly in the grass directly below where she had disappeared. She kept watching closely for any stomping feet that could squish her before she could carry out the second step of her plan. When she was fairly sure that the majority of thieves were in the open space between the smaller tents and the larger one, she tested her delicate wings, then lifted off the ground, her whole body vibrating with a buzz.

Of course, the men would barely notice her. Who would bother with a busy, little bee? As she buzzed, she felt an amazing sense of power, and then as she rose into the air, something shifted in her mind. It was like a door opened in her imagination, and the view in her mind's eye was limit-less. There were endless possibilities. If the power to change was linked to the imagination— but a shout from a pursuer nearby startled her. Morgan came back to where she was, remembering her plan, and knowing she had to stay focused.

Flying over to the edge of the open space, Morgan made sure she was as far from the group of men as she could get, but still in their sight. Then another flash of light, a rumble of thunder, and she changed into a tabby cat with flaming orange fur.

All heads jerked immediately in her direction, and the leader jabbed his finger toward her.

"Capture that cat!" he roared.

A couple of his men were confused, and others clearly thought their leader had gone crazy, but nearly all of them responded to his orders, if only because he was so angry.

As Morgan turned to flee, she caught sight of the wolf sneaking into the large tent behind the bald leader. Then she was off! Morgan led the group of thieves all around the camp, weaving in and out of the small tents, making sure most of the men were following her before she began phase three of her plan.

She ran behind the line of horses tied to the corral fence near the river. Meowing loudly and leaping high, she landed on one of the horse's backs. Then she leaped down the line from one horse's back to the other. The horses panicked. They flung their heads around wildly and discovered they were no longer tied up.

This was due, of course, to the earliest part of Morgan's plan. Sneaking to untie the horses had been easy for Rusty and Morgan, since the thieves tended to be lazy, and didn't pay much attention to their animals.

It was now time for the last part of her plan, and Morgan's heart pounded as she ran. Even though she had practiced part of this final step before, there was always the possibility that she would run out of energy and not be able to carry it through. The early summer run-off in the river roared, reminding her of the great power she was about to face.

As the group of thieves came after her, she ran straight up a maple tree near the river. She climbed out on a branch that almost reached the water's edge. When she was sure most of them had their eyes on her, she sprung high off the branch, a long leap that took her out over the riverbank and into the raging waters below.

She was still in her tabby form, and the freezing water caught her in a fast current which sent her in a tumble, rushing, rushing downstream. She had no breath. She had no more energy. Having given everything she had, she was now lost to the rush of cold water. She began to sink, lower and lower toward the bottom of the river. The light was beginning to dim when she felt a jolt from the area of her chest. It awakened her enough that she made one last effort.

To Morgan, the change that took place seemed to happen over a very long time. Instead of a flash of light, Morgan saw what looked like a bolt of lightning cut through the gloomy water.

As if in a dream, the light coming out of her moved infinitely slowly, growing like a tree with bright branches. The light **created an endless pattern, which repeated itself over and over in a similar but smaller form**—until the glow was lost in the murk of the dark water.

With a rush of oxygen, Morgan realized that she could finally breathe. She opened her gills wider and let the oxygen in the water revive her. She'd wanted the men to see a cat caught in the rushing waters so that they would come after her, but she had not foreseen the blast of the chill water, and the furious force of the river. Shivering, she felt with a deeper chill how close she had come to giving up.

She decided to stay as a small trout, resting way below the surface on the stony river bottom, so that she could regain her strength.

As she lay there, she saw large bodies thrash past her above. Many thieves and even some panicked horses had been caught by the wild river and flung further downstream.

Finally, she began to gather both her strength and her wits. She and Rusty had tried to calculate how long it would take the rescuers to arrive at the camp. Rusty said that the wagon could only travel about five miles per hour. With ten miles to cover, she and Rusty had estimated that the searchers would arrive about an hour later than they had. The children had timed the escape as best as they could, hoping that the rescuers would find the camp when it was in the most turmoil. That way, the rescuers would have a chance of overcoming the thieves.

Hope filled her. Hope that Rusty and Grandpa Allen had escaped. Hope that maybe even now they'd be meeting up with the rescue party. With the rush of feeling, hope sprung from deeper within—hope that her father was alive—that he was, even now, returning to them.

No matter how much she wanted to keep resting, Morgan realized that she couldn't just stay here at the river bottom. Too long, and she might not be able to make it back upstream. Rusty would meet her near Harlow, after secretly making sure Grandpa Allen was well on his way home. Gliding against the flow of the river, Morgan began to swim.

❦

Long afterward—it seemed like lifetimes later—Morgan was wiggling her way upstream when she saw a familiar face with red curling hair waiting for her by the river's edge. He'd taken off his shoes and was standing in a shallow eddy watching for her. She swam near his feet, which were magnified in the clear water. She didn't remember deciding to shift form, but there was a flash followed by a rumble, and then everything faded —until there was nothing—nothing at all.

Chapter Twelve

FINDING HOME

*"Where we love is home—
home that our feet may leave
but not our hearts."*

Oliver Wendell Holmes

SOFT words. Clock ticking. Warmth along her back. Pale light. Gentle hands on her forehead. The drift of sounds and senses gathered in time to a single point, and Morgan woke. Late afternoon light warmed her arms and coverlet underneath. Morgan tried to roll onto her back, and Jip yelped and sat up. Rusty walked into view and stood next to the bedpost, then moved aside the silk hangings to sit on the bed next to her.

"Can you hear me now?" he asked quietly.

Morgan nodded her head. She still felt hazy, and her body felt sore all over. Rusty looked relieved.

"How long?" Morgan croaked.

"Two days," replied Rusty. "I promised your mother and Grandpa Allen that I would get them right away."

Morgan put her hand on his and squeezed. "Please, just a moment. I want to know what happened. And there are things I can't ask with my mother here."

She tried to sit up but decided that lying back down felt much better.

"Water?" she croaked again.

Rusty stood and picked up a glass from the side table. The water tasted wonderful, like the best thing she had ever put in her mouth.

"Your mother was so worried," Rusty told her. "She thought you were in a coma or something."

"Grandpa Allen?" Morgan asked.

"He told her you were tough as bones and not to worry, that you'd pull through," Rusty smiled. "He's fine too. He complained more about the bumpy ride back in the wagon than he did about being kidnapped."

Morgan smiled. Her brow creased as she thought. "The thieves?"

"Mostly rounded up by the rescue party. They are sitting in jail in Harlow," Rusty explained. "Probably, they'll be in a work gang within a few weeks."

Morgan took a moment to look around. She realized she was in the beautiful bedroom.

"Why am I here?" she asked.

"You blacked out, and I ran to get help from Harlow, 'cause the rescue party had already left with Grandpa Allen. The good people there helped me bring you home, and Grandpa Allen and I snuck you up here before your mother knew you were gone. Anyway, Grandpa Allen was angry when he learned that Miss Stern had put you and your mother in basement rooms. No one lives down there because it's too cold. He moved your mother into the room next door to this one." Rusty looked around. "So, this is your room now."

"But what about Grandpa Allen?" Morgan protested.

"Oh, this wasn't his room," Rusty explained, "This room belonged to my Grandma, and Grandpa Allen said you should have it. He says it's the least he could do, seeing how you saved his life and all."

"But I didn't save his life!" said Morgan.

"That's how he sees it—you and I, we're big heroes in his eyes," Rusty told her. "Of course, we can't tell anyone else about it, but he said he'll always know."

Rusty stood up off the bed. "You rest sleepyhead. I'll go get them."

Rusty left, and while she waited, Morgan gazed around the bedroom. It was hard to believe that it was hers now. A fire crackled in the fireplace, and the afternoon sun streamed in, washing the room in golden light. She glanced over at the vanity mirror to one side of the bed. She even had a secret passage leading right from her bedroom.

Come to think of it that could work both ways. Someone could get in as well, like the thieves. She would have to talk to Grandpa Allen about an alarm system and a lock for the door leading into the tunnel.

As she snuggled down in the covers and hugged Jip, the door burst open. Morgan's mother, Grandpa Allen, Rusty, and a maid carrying a tray of food came in and surrounded her bed. They all began talking at once, and Morgan smiled as she looked at all their faces. She was so lucky and so grateful to be here with them. There was a time in the stream when she almost didn't make it. Morgan shuddered and put that thought aside as she slowly sat up.

Dara was feeling her forehead, and Grandpa Allen winked at her and gave her a thumbs up. The maid set the tray of food across her lap: vegetable soup, hot biscuits, baked pear, and Boston cream pie. Morgan started eating eagerly, and her mother sat back, watching with relief. Suddenly Dara leaned forward and kissed Morgan on the top of her head. Morgan stopped eating and reached forward to hug her mother tight. When Dara finally sat back, she swiped quickly at her eyes. Then trying to pull herself back together, Dara asked the maid where the tea was, and they both left to retrieve enough for all of them.

Rusty sat on the bed, and Grandpa Allen pulled up a chair. They sat quietly for a moment, letting Morgan eat.

Grandpa Allen cleared his throat. "I wanted to thank you, my dear, for everything you did for me. Rusty told me the details of the rescue you two carried out together. I was particularly impressed with your planning and control. To succeed with four such complex and different creatures in so short a time," he shook his head. "It is far beyond what I thought was possible."

"And I'm just waiting for you to teach me," added Rusty.

Grandpa Allen grew more serious. "While I am very grateful, I am also aware that you took a great risk, and if the past few days teach us anything, it's that the risk was nearly too much." He paused to gaze at Morgan closely.

She wanted to deny it, but she hesitated. She knew that he was right. She had nearly gone too far.

Grandpa Allen could see that she understood him. "I accept this time that the situation was extreme. Let us hope that we will not find ourselves in such a position again."

Morgan put down her fork. "I do have one important question."

"Ask it, my dear," said Grandpa Allen.

She turned to Rusty, "You said the thieves were mostly rounded up. Did that include their leader?"

"Very quick of you, child," said Grandpa Allen. "I told Rusty not to discuss it with you right away. I wanted to give you some time to recover from your ordeal, but no, the leader was never found."

"Do you think he'll be back?" Morgan asked.

"Not for a time. He's lost a great deal," replied Grandpa Allen. "But I know him very well, and he does not give up easily. Ever since we were young, it was clear that he could be very single-minded."

"You knew him?" Morgan asked. She looked from Rusty to Grandpa Allen, confused.

"The original leader died some years ago, child. The leader now was raised by him—from quite a young age, and he grew to follow in his footsteps."

Grandpa Allen looked from one child to the other. "We will continue to guard the secret of the medallion together, and I am grateful beyond words to have you two by my side."

Morgan felt proud that she was now part of something so important. She looked over at Rusty, and they smiled at one another.

Then Grandpa Allen continued, almost talking to himself, "I thought I would never see him again, but I never dreamed that when I did, I would not be overjoyed as I'd always imagined."

Oh No! Morgan thought, and she gasped out loud.

Grandpa Allen studied her gravely, "I can see you have already guessed what I discovered. I'm afraid everything is much more difficult and personal for me now."

"Wait. . . What?" Rusty asked.

Morgan looked at Grandpa Allen, and he gave her a small, sad nod. She turned to Rusty, knowing without a doubt that she was right.

"The man who is after the medallion, the bald leader. . ." she explained, "He's Grandpa Allen's long-lost brother."

MEDALLION MATTERS

THIS section is for those kids and adults who want to delve deeper into the subjects found in the Morgan series. Every time you see a Medallion at the end of a sentence, you can go to this section to find out more fun facts.

1. *"Did you know that almost all flowers have a certain number of petals?"* he would ask. *"There is a pattern to the numbers they have. If you put the numbers in a sequence, they go like this: 3, 5, 8, 13, 21, 34, 55, 89. . ."*

The Fibonacci Sequence

Morgan's father talks about the number of petals most flowers have and how those numbers create a sequence that has a pattern. This number series is part of a math concept called the "Fibonacci numbers" or the "Fibonacci sequence." The Fibonacci sequence isn't usually taught until middle school or high school, so please don't feel discouraged if it seems difficult. Many adults struggle with figuring out the pattern, as well!

3, 5, 8, 13, 21, 34, 55, 89

Hint: Try adding the first two numbers and see what you get.

Answer: When you add two numbers in the sequence, they equal the next number in the series. The "Fibonacci sequence" was discovered over eight hundred years ago by an Italian mathematician named Leonardo Pisano. He was also called Fibonacci, which, according to some texts, means the son of Bonacci. Leonardo Pisano was inspired and influenced by the work of much earlier math scholars in the Middle East and Southeast Asia.

Amazingly, this number series is found over and over again in nature. We can find the Fibonacci sequence in the number of petals on most flowers, in the spirals of seeds in a sunflower, or a pinecone, and in the spiral of chambers of a nautilus shell. Living things in nature grow according to this sequence because it is the most efficient way for them to flourish. This series of numbers unlocks many of the math mysteries in the universe.

2. Her father and a team of scientists were there to follow in the footsteps of a man her father described as "one of the greatest thinkers of our time."

Charles Darwin

When Morgan's father talks about following in the footsteps of "one of the greatest thinkers of our time," he is talking about following in the footsteps of Charles Darwin.

Darwin was born in 1809 in Britain. He was a naturalist and an explorer who visited the Galapagos Islands more than sixty years earlier than Morgan's father. The Galapagos Islands are off the coast of Ecuador in South America.

Charles Darwin observed nature very carefully, and he developed a scientific theory about the way that animals change their features and traits over many generations.

His theory is that species evolve over time due to a process of natural selection. If their traits adapt better to their environment, then they and their offspring will have a better chance of survival over multiple generations.

3. *"This is called a **Magic Square**," Rusty said, pointing down to the garden. "The 'magic' is in the way the numbers—the number of bushes that is—work so well together. Can you see why?" Rusty asked.*

Magic Squares

Magic Squares have been around for thousands of years. In the first century A.D., a Chinese legend describes the first magic square appearing on the back of a turtle climbing out from a river.

A U.S. founding father, Benjamin Franklin, created amazing magic squares. He lived during the 1700s, and he was an author, philosopher, scientist, politician, diplomat, printer, inventor, and musician, and supposedly, he hated math! Yet he accomplished his magic squares without the aid of a computer.

4. *"An abolitionist was a person who wanted the slaves to be free," explained Rusty. "The slaves would escape from their masters and move from safe place to safe place. All the houses and farms along the way were known as the* **Underground Railroad.**"

Underground Railroad

The Underground Railroad was a series of secret routes and safe places that slaves could travel from the southern states to the North, where they would be free. The slaves usually stopped traveling when they reached a northern state where they would not be persecuted. Some slaves traveled all the way to Canada.

Although there were hidden passageways in some houses along the Underground Railroad, most of the Underground Railroad was not really hidden or under the ground. Some people who helped the slaves escape did have secret rooms or tunnels, but usually, the slaves traveled under cover of night and stayed in the houses of the abolitionist families. The Underground Railroad ran roughly from the late 1780s until the end of the Civil War.

5. *"It's a telegram sent to Grandpa Allen," she said, showing it to Morgan. "It's from the **Department of Zoology at Stanford University**. They are the ones heading the expedition to the Galapagos."*

Stanford Expeditions to the Galapagos

```
Western United Telegram Company
            CABLE SERVICE ACROSS THE GLOBE.
        HIRAM WADE, PRESIDENT AND GENERAL MANAGER

RECEIVED at   BOSTON MASS.                              1899

  12 Shipwrecked survivorsfound near Chatham  Island
  Plantation.Good possibility they are from the
  Hopkins-Stanford GalapagosExpedition.  No word of
  identities yet. Will keep you informed as news arrives.
                   Robert E. Snodgrass
             Professor, Departmentof Zoology
                  Stanford University
```

There really was an expedition to the Galapagos Islands from 1898 to 1899. The exploration was led by scientists from Stanford University who left on a ship out of San Francisco. Robert E. Snodgrass was actually one of the scientists on the expedition who collected animals and plants. There were no shipwrecks during the real expedition.

6. *As if in a dream, the light coming out of her moved infinitely slowly, growing like a tree with bright branches.* **The light created an endless pattern, which repeated itself over and over in a similar but smaller form**—*until the glow was lost in the murk of the dark water.*

Fractals

The image Morgan sees rising from her chest is a bolt of lightning. The pattern that she sees, which is repeated over and over in smaller form in an endless pattern, is what mathematicians and scientists call a FRACTAL. There are all kinds of fractals in the world. Many of them can be found in nature, such as the seeds of a pine cone, the chambers of a nautilus seashell, or the seeds of a sunflower.

Made in the USA
Lexington, KY
29 October 2019